SCARECROW SEASON

Jack Verneski

SCARECROW SEASON

First Edition

First Printing 2012

ISBN-13: 978-0-9845777-4-3

Technical Review Editor: Nelson O. Ottenhausen
Managing Editor: Dari Bradley
Sr. Editor: Doris Littlefield

Published by Patriot Media, Inc.
Publishing America's Patriots

P.O. Box 5414
Niceville, FL 32578
United States of America
www.patriotmediainc.com

Acknowledgements

First, I thank the Patriot Media family, especially Dari Bradley and Nelson Ottenhausen, for believing in my story and for all their help in bringing it to completion.

My profound thanks to my daughter Apolla and her husband Scott for giving me their support and providing a lot of needed computer assistance.

And finally, I would be remiss if I didn't acknowledge all the Air Force ground-pounders who inspired me. I salute you.

Introduction

During a forty year period after World War II, beginning in 1946 until the late 1980s, the United States and the Union of Soviet Socialist Republics (USSR) became engaged in a political conflict known as the Cold War, primarily a disagreement over the world control of nuclear power, especially military weapons. Each country prepared to defend themselves against a nuclear attack from the other and in the process, military buildups became the norm. Both superpowers realized in order to survive an all-out first strike, they had to create effective deterrent measures as well as having a military defensive system, and thus the United States began building up the Air Force to protect the country against Russian nuclear submarines, intercontinental missiles and long range bombers.

During the early 1960s, an all-weather interceptor aircraft, the Convair F-106 Delta Dart, also known as the *Six,* came into the Air Force inventory as part of the Aerospace Defense Command (ADC) with the primary mission to shoot down Russian aircraft using specialized missiles. The F-106 also had the capacity to carry nuclear munitions. After twenty years of service, the Air Force retired the F-106.

I didn't know it at the time I reported to my assignment as a maintenance officer in the 50th Fighter Interceptor Squadron of Aerospace Defense Command, but the ADC bore the brunt of defending the United States homeland with a fourteen-year-old primary ADC interceptor, the F-106 Delta Dart.

Six years before I reported for duty, plans called for replacing the F-106 (considered ancient by Air Force standards at that time) with a new interceptor—the much heralded F-4. People who knew airplanes said, "The new interceptor is *something else.*" The new bird would be a maintenance man's dream—the culmination of lessons learned through countless hours of flight and maintenance with the F-106 and its earlier predecessors.

But during that time, the war in Vietnam evolved much bigger than expected and plans changed. The Russian MIG-21 began to appear in Southeast Asia, and Tactical Air Command (TAC) needed an aircraft to match its capabilities. Almost overnight, while still in the design stage, Department of Defense converted the F-4 into an air superiority and attack fighter to fill the needs of TAC. The generals in ADC objected vigorously, but to no avail because Southeast Asia had priority and ADC, no longer the bright, new boy in the United States Air Force, had to make do with the F-106.

Not only did ADC lose an aircraft, but during a six year period it lost most of its experienced pilots and maintenance personnel to TAC. To breach the gap, the Dart underwent a series of structural modifications to extend its active life to an astonishing 8000 flight hours, much more than any other first-line interceptor and certainly more than the designers ever intended. Hoping for better days ahead, the Air Force changed Air Defense Command to Aerospace Defense Command.

I knew the Air Force took a calculated risk at a time when the concept of continental air defense began changing rapidly—missiles and submarines were in vogue, not manned interceptors. The primary responsibility for nuclear deterrence had changed.

When I reported to Olefield Air Force Base in the fall of 1971, the political pot began to boil and in 1972, a presidential election year, certain political factions would have to be convinced that our continental air defense capabilities had not deteriorated because of expenditures in Southeast Asia. The *old* Dart would be called on for service beyond the call of duty, and the airmen of ADC would have challenges no one anticipated.

Prologue

The F-106 Delta Dart had just completed a perfect training intercept on a designated target aircraft and headed back to base in Montana. Captain Billy Bob Hammond, an experienced pilot of 13 years, had less than a year in the Dart and for him, the transition to the delta wing aircraft became a big adjustment, especially landings, because the aircraft had a tendency to drop quickly.

On the September morning in 1971, during takeoff an hour and a half earlier, Captain Hammond noticed the runway a little slick.

After takeoff, an internal flight control system, along with a sophisticated ground based radar system, took over the F-106 and guided it to the correct attack position and achieved a successful intercept. He didn't fire any weapons on this training mission.

Captain Hammond felt pleased.

The automatic control system had the capability to return the aircraft to the vicinity of the base, and Captain Hammond let the aircraft take him home. He took the opportunity to relax a little and his mind drifted to other things in his life, his twin six-year-old daughters who just started school, and the party his wife planned for the weekend with a few other pilots and their wives.

As the aircraft approached the base, Captain Hammond knew he faced a challenging approach and landing on the short, slippery runway. He had to stop thinking about family and friends.

Pilots loved flying the beautiful, sleek *Six* because of the power and response it offered, unmatched by any other aircraft in the inventory. The only criticism made by the pilots, "too hot" to handle sometimes or "too hard to slow down". Because of its delta wing design it had no flaps to help slow it down when landing.

As Captain Hammond neared the base, he took control of the aircraft. Actually, it could land itself, but no self respecting pilot would allow that to happen.

Less than two years earlier, in the winter of 1970, one of the squadron pilots lost control of his aircraft at altitude and found himself in a dangerous flat spin. He decided to eject and the F-106 recovered and made a belly landing, undamaged, in a snow covered farmer's field. The news media referred to the incident as the Cornfield Bomber.

Captain Hammond focused as he rolled out on final at a little over 1500 feet. A visible light snow covered the runway and a poorly designed canopy and an old weathered windshield made for poor visibility. The captain worked the throttle hard to control the airspeed and rate of descent. With an approach at 325 knots, he opened the speed brakes and shortly afterwards, at 250 knots, the landing gear lowered. Because of the slick conditions and short runway, Captain Hammond planned to land short on the runway to allow for a long roll.

The F-106 would land at about 180 knots, which translates to over 200 mph and only a small margin for error. The excitement of coming in just above ground level, with a short runway and poor conditions, created a *high* that only a *Six* pilot would know.

As he approached the end of the runway, Captain Hammond worked the throttle to achieve the proper attitude for flare-out—then it happened—the power of the big engine shut down.

He didn't sense the power loss until too late and had no time to try a restart or even eject. The F-106 dropped fast and the impact on the hard Montana ground killed Captain Hammond. The aircraft came apart just short of the runway, scattering pieces over acres.

Captain Hammond had almost made it home.

The accident investigation team arrived the next morning and began the tedious job of determining the cause of the crash. It took a week to find and recover all the aircraft parts. The severely damaged engine could not be properly examined and after several weeks, the preliminary report indicated the accident's cause as *undetermined.*

Accident notification bulletins went out to every F-106 squadron guarding the boundaries of the United States against a Russian bomber attack. Major Harry Bensen, Chief of Maintenance at the 50th fighter interceptor squadron on Cape Cod read the bulletin carefully and with concern. To the old WWII veteran, the tail number seemed more familiar to him than the pilot's name.

SCARECROW SEASON

Cast of Characters

Barry	Captain, head of Base Air Police
Bean	Airman, Crew Chief of 251 & 255
Bensen, Harry	Major, Chief of Maintenance,
Biggs	Master Sergeant, Night Shift
Braddock	General, Base Commander
Breathstone	Colonel, CO 69th Fighter Interceptor Squadron
Buckley	Airman, alias *Scarecrow One*
Clymer	Crew Chief
Conn	Sergeant, Maintenance Control
Cummings, Alfred	Tech Sergeant, T-Bird Flight Chief
Depolo	Sergeant, B-Flight Chief
Fox	Sergeant, Electrical Shop
Fritz	Airman
Grobly	Sergeant, A-Flight Chief
Hardesty	Airman
Hardy	Airman, Crew Chief
Harkins	Airman, Crew Chief of 415
Harmon	Major, Operations Officer
Harrington, Joe	Lieutenant, Maintenance Officer
Harris	Lieutenant, Pilot
Higgins	Airman
Holt, Tim	Lieutenant, Pilot

Janice	Secretary to Colonel Wyler
Johnson, Bill	Captain, Pilot & Squadron Historian
Jones, (Jonsey)	Sergeant, NCO, Sheet Metal Shop
Jones, Percy	Airman, Drag Chute Shop
Kelly	Airman
Lickle	Captain, Pilot & Flight Safety Officer
Panza	Airman, Crew Chief of 381
Pardini, Joseph	Sergeant, NCO, Records, Reports & Analysis
Paris	Sergeant, Drag Chute Shop
Parkinson	Airman, Crew Chief
Parks	Lieutenant, Pilot
Roberts, Frank	Captain, Armament Officer, Nuclear Arsenal
Rosenberg, (Rosy)	Airman, Squadron Supply
Seimons, (Joe)	Captain, Pilot & Maintenance Officer
Shock, (Will)	Warrant Officer, Electronics
Shilling	Airman, Supply
Singly	Sergeant, Engine Shop
Spencer	Colonel, ORI Leader
Sterling, Nobel	Chief Master Sergeant, Line Chief
Swartz	Airman, T-Bird Crew Chief
Taft, Elmer	Sergeant, Squadron Supply
Talifano	Master Sergeant, First Sergeant
Tench	Sergeant, Electronic Shops
Thompson, Buzz	Lieutenant Commander, Navy Exchange Pilot
Tiddyings	Airman, Instrument Technician
Townley	Chief Master Sergeant, Line Chief
Williams, Percy	Airman, File Clerk, Records
Wyler	Colonel, 50th Squadron Commander

Dedication

I dedicate this book to my wife Joyce, my daughter Apolla and to the memory of my brother Casimer, a United States Air Force veteran.

SCARECROW SEASON

Chapter 1

Scarecrow Squadron

As far back as I can remember, I dreamed of becoming a fighter pilot in the United States Air Force. When the Air Force notified me that I had been accepted for flight training, I felt excited and proud. Two weeks after graduating from college, I reported to Vance Air Force Base in Oklahoma, a reserve second lieutenant determined to be the best pilot in the Air Force.

Two months later the dream came to an end. I washed out, a dismal failure.

On the day I left Vance, my flight instructor, a dark-haired, friendly captain, stopped by the barracks and said, “Good luck, Harrington, I guess you’re just a paradox.”

He was right. On the ground, I tested first in my class and flew the Link Trainer like a twenty-year veteran, but in the air something weird happened. The moment the captain said, “You got it, Harrington,” and took his hand off the stick, I became disoriented, unable to find the runway even when it was right under the aircraft.

My mother felt happy I wouldn’t be flying. She said I would have killed myself if they ever let me solo.

A personnel officer at Vance told me I would make a good navigator, but I wasn't so sure anymore and instead, I decided to go to Chanute Air Force Base, Illinois, to learn aircraft maintenance. After three months of maintenance school and thirty days of requested early leave, I found myself reporting to my first assignment, as a maintenance officer in the 50th Fighter Interceptor Squadron. My destination this time—the Air Defense Command at Olefield Air Force Base, Cape Cod, Massachusetts.

In October 1971, I drove through Buzzards Bay then over the Bourne Bridge and on to Cape Cod. The salty air filled my nostrils. In contrast to the brilliant autumn colors on the mainland, scrub pine and sand surrounded the Cape highway to Olefield. As I approached the main gate, I reflected on the war raging in Vietnam and my good fortune in having received such a choice location as Cape Cod. I stopped my little overcrowded sports car at the main entrance, and the AP (Air Police) guard snapped a sharp salute.

After checking my orders, he said, "The 50th is straight ahead, Lieutenant. Just keep going through the base on the same road."

"Thanks."

The road wound its way through the large base and as I drove, I felt the cardboard box pressing into my side. It had been there all through the trip from Pennsylvania, a silly little gift given to me by my maintenance contemporaries at Chanute when they learned of my assignment to ADC. They crammed it full of thoughtful things—a tube of Elmer's Glue-All, a ball of string, assorted rubber bands and Band-Aids just to mention a few of the items someone thought I might be able to make use of in maintenance.

I drove through the heart of the base, past a lot of old, World War II type Army barracks and then by a squadron of SAC (Strategic Air command) tankers. Finally, I approached what had to be the area of the 50th. Four huge, gray maintenance hangars loomed like elephants, two on each side of a little yellow Operations building. Driving into the squadron, I passed under an arched sign which read: Welcome to the 50th Fighter Interceptor Squadron, Home of the Fighting Scarecrows.

As I entered the two-story Operations building, a pilot in a bright orange flight suit gave me directions to the commander's office on the second floor. I climbed the steps and looked into a little anteroom connected to the CO's office. A young, attractive, civilian secretary sat typing. She had long blonde hair, a creamy complexion and her angelic smile welcomed me to the squadron.

"I'm Lieutenant Joe Harrington, reporting for duty," I said.

"Hi, I'm Janice," she said with a sweet friendly voice. "Please have a seat. Colonel Wyler will see you soon." Then she whispered, "He's wrestling with Major Harmon, the operations officer."

I could hear a heated conversation taking place in the colonel's office over the dull hum of the typing and assumed the colonel said, "This is the third morning in a row that maintenance hasn't provided enough aircraft, Major."

"I'm well aware of that, Colonel, but Harry ... uh ... I mean Major Bensen gave me only eight birds."

"What's his excuse today?"

The major replied, "I don't know. He just said they had some unusual problems last night."

Colonel Wyler yelled, "Unusual problems, my ass," causing Janice's creamy complexion to turn a little rosy. "Excuses, that's all we get from Bensen. We've already missed our quota of sorties and flying hours for the month. Our purpose here is to train pilots and fly airplanes to protect the United States."

"As operations officer I'm well aware of that, Colonel. All I need are operationally ready aircraft. Besides, what if an inspection team dropped in on us right now?"

"Did you call Maintenance Control?"

"No, sir. Major Bensen throws a fit when you go over his head."

The colonel yelled, "Bullshit! Do you know why Three-sixty-three (363) missed the first flight yesterday?"

"No, sir."

"Well I do. The crew chief couldn't find the forms. That's the kind of unusual problems Major Bensen has. Okay, you can go. I guess I'll have to talk to Bensen again."

An overweight major with a red face hurried through the anteroom then Janice rose. As she entered the colonel's office, I noticed she had a petite and shapely figure.

I heard her say, "Colonel, there's a new lieutenant reporting in."

He replied, "Have him come in. Also, tell Sergeant Talifano I want to see him."

I took two military steps inside the office, snapped to attention and saluted. "Lieutenant Harrington, reporting for duty, sir!"

"At ease, Lieutenant … have a seat."

I sat on a leather couch while Colonel Wyler remained standing. After listening from the anteroom, I expected to see a giant. Instead, before me stood a short, thin man with a close-cropped, blonde crew cut which gave him a boyish appearance.

"It's certainly good to have you in the squadron, Lieutenant," he said while reviewing my records.

"It's nice to be here, sir," I answered.

"I see you just graduated from Maintenance Officers School."

"Yes, sir," I said proudly.

"Some flying experience too," he said, sounding impressed.

"Yes, sir."

"That's good."

He passed in front of me, and I watched my reflection dance in his spit-shined shoes. "I'm sort of new here too, Lieutenant. Came here three months ago from SAC. Started in Korea and then into bombers. This is my first command."

As I sat and listened to the colonel relate his distinguished career, I surveyed the spacious office. Over the desk hung many awards he had received from SAC, along with a beautifully framed diploma from West Point. In the opposite corner stood the American flag beside a huge glass case filled with golfing trophies. A new picture window overlooked the entire aircraft parking apron.

"Well, that's enough of the past," the colonel said. "Getting back to the squadron, there's a lot of work to be done and you can be a big help, Lieutenant. I don't mind telling you that maintenance is too loose … no discipline. I get the impression the airmen do as they please … there's no supervisory control. With your background and training, Lieutenant, you can help make this a real military outfit."

"I hope so, sir."

"Good. Well, I guess you're anxious to get to work. I'll have Janice get Major Bensen, our chief of maintenance. Good luck."

"Thank you, sir."

As I walked out of the office, I passed a chief master sergeant, poised and waiting to enter. His robust frame and crooked nose made him look mean. On his left chest he wore more service ribbons than I had ever seen before.

Janice said, "He's the squadron's first sergeant and has the next office down the hall."

Major Bensen stood waiting downstairs in the pilots' mess. In a well-worn, orange flight suit, he looked about six-foot-three and somewhere in his fifties. This came as a surprise because I expected a major to be much younger. A greasy, blue Air Force cap sat on the back of his head, displaying a mass of disheveled gray hair. As a complement, he sported a gray bushy mustache.

We shook hands, a firm, solid union, then sat at one of the empty tables in the mess.

Major Bensen slouched back and took a long puff on an old corncob pipe. "How was maintenance school?"

"Just fine, sir."

"Did you learn anything?"

The question caught me by surprise. "A lot of maintenance procedures and practices, sir. The class I was in even did a complete periodic inspection on an aircraft." He didn't seem too impressed so I added, "I guess we didn't learn a heck of a lot about airplanes."

The major sat up, leaned on the table, and said with a grin that put me more at ease, "That's okay." He had a penetrating look and brown, sensitive eyes.

But it sounded all too familiar and I recalled my first day in flight school. The instructor asked for a show of hands from all those who had flown before. After half the class proudly raised their hands, he said, "Well, that's too bad because you guys have a lot to relearn." As it turned out only those with prior flying experience made it.

Major Bensen asked, "What did they teach you about people?"

"People?"

"That's right."

"Nothing, sir," I said. "What's there to know about people?"

Major Bensen looked at me as if to say I didn't mean what I had said. "People are a maintenance officer's job, Joe. Call it human engineering if you want to give it a fancy name. I've been in the Air

Force almost twenty-nine years now, and if there's one thing I've learned, it's that only people make any real difference."

"I can't argue with that, sir. It would be like arguing against motherhood or the flag."

"Let's take it one step further then," he said. "What do you think makes a man want to contribute something … to do his best?"

"Oh … I'd say pride, and I'd guess satisfaction in his work."

"Good! Now we're getting somewhere," he said with a gleam in his brown eyes. "Those are the keys to a maintenance officer's job, Joe. It's our responsibility to create an atmosphere which recognizes the dignity and importance of each man, so that he can achieve personal satisfaction and at the same time contribute something. I know it sounds a little corny, but only under such conditions will an airman develop the capacity to exercise his creativity and ingenuity, and believe me, we need those things in maintenance now more than ever before."

"It sounds like you're for a lot of individual initiative."

"I am."

"The colonel told me he thought we needed more control."

"Yes, I know. I didn't say it was going to be easy, did I?"

"No, sir."

"Well, it's not, but I'm sure we can handle it," Major Bensen said, and I thought I detected a hint of mischief in his voice. Then he added, "Come on, it's about time for the first launch."

We walked out the back door of operations and stopped to watch from the edge of the apron. I counted eight F-106 interceptors on the line with a few pilots already in the cockpits while others continued their preflights with the crew chiefs. A little, blue pickup truck moved slowly behind the line of aircraft.

The major said, "That's Chief Master Sergeant Townley in the truck. He's the line chief."

At exactly 8:30 the first two aircraft started up then began to taxi to the runway. The line chief moved the pickup near the next two and stopped. Major Bensen stood with his hands folded across his chest. A crew chief plugged the power cable into tail number 380. But when the engine started, fuel poured out of several vents under the fuselage. Major Bensen only watched as the line chief jumped from the truck, ran to the aircraft and pulled out the power cable.

The siphoning stopped.

"That's something new," said Major Bensen.

I noticed a worried expression on his weathered face.

The next aircraft, tail number 259, started up and proceeded to the runway. Meanwhile the ground crew made another attempt on 380, but again the fuel poured out when the engine started. Ready this time, the crew chief yanked the power cable, stopping the siphon. We watched as the pilot slowly unbuckled then climbed down the ladder, aborting the flight. He walked toward us with his gear over one shoulder.

The first two aircraft reached a distant runway and began their take-off rolls simultaneously. Partway down the runway, both their afterburners blasted the still morning and the sudden explosion frightened off a small flock of seagulls at the end of the runway.

"Believe it or not, the base dump is right off of One-eighty-two (182)," Major Bensen said. "For years we've been trying to get the base commander to move it somewhere else."

"No luck?"

"No, it just keeps getting bigger."

Both aircraft roared into the sky and became smaller and smaller until only two dots remained—then nothing. The pilot who aborted 380, passed close by, waving to the major with his free hand.

I recognized his navy uniform so I asked, "What's the Navy doing here?"

"That's Lieutenant Commander Thompson … Buzz. He's on exchange duty. Good pilot … Naval Academy graduate."

Then Colonel Wyler went by carrying his helmet and gear.

As if possessed, he stopped suddenly, turned and yelled, "I'd like to see you in my office when I get down, Major."

"Sure thing, Colonel."

The colonel proceeded to aircraft 401 and began his preflight, a tall crew chief at his side. Two more aircraft reached the runway and boomed off. Finally the colonel climbed into the cockpit, ready to go. But instead of the characteristic whine of the jet, the colonel signaled for the crew chief to climb up the ladder. The line chief seemed unconcerned and remained in the truck.

"It's the windshield," Major Bensen said with a funny smirk. "The colonel has this thing about windshields. They're all pretty old and dirt gets imbedded in the scratches."

We watched as the colonel talked, pointing to the lower section of the windshield. The crew chief nodded until the CO finished. Finally, the engine roared and the aircraft headed for the runway.

The blue pickup turned and came in our direction. Beside the line chief, it looked like someone slouched down in the other seat. The truck stopped abruptly and the line chief hopped out.

Major Bensen said, "Lieutenant Joe Harrington, meet Chief Master Sergeant Townley. Joe is a new maintenance officer."

"Nice to meet you, Lieutenant. Welcome aboard."

A rugged built man with a big chest and slim waist, Sergeant Townley wore a leather baseball cap with a scarecrow insignia pulled tightly on his head to be sure a jet engine wouldn't gobble it up. He wore clean and pressed olive green fatigues, except for a wet spot on the right pant leg where fuel from aircraft 380 spilled on it.

Seeing the young airman slouched in the passenger's seat with his head down and covered from head to foot with black soot, Major Bensen asked, "Problems, Sarge?"

"Yes, sir," Sergeant Townley replied. "During the preflight, Lieutenant Holt made Hardy here climb through the afterburner to check the turbine blades."

Major Bensen ran his hand through his mop of gray hair. "Okay, I'll take care of it."

"I'm not crying, Major," Sergeant Townley said, "but this is the second time this month that kid, I mean pilot, made one of the crew chiefs check the blades. If I wasn't occupied with Three-eighty (380), I would've caught him. You know I always have the graveyard shift check the blades."

"Right … I know, Sarge, I'll take care of the matter."

Sergeant Townley jumped back into the truck and said. "It's a good thing Talifano didn't see him like this."

Major Bensen nodded and leaned on the door. "Sarge, can you take Lieutenant Harrington over to see the alert barn this afternoon?"

"Sure, be glad to. About one o'clock, Lieutenant?"

"Fine."

"Meet you right here then."

Sergeant Townley drove away and I followed Major Bensen to the center of the apron. When we turned around, I had a panoramic view of the squadron area. The first thing that caught my eye was the colonel's big picture window straight ahead.

"Some window!"

"Yes, he had it installed right after he got here. Someone told him he wouldn't be welcome in maintenance. I wonder where they ever got that idea," Major Bensen said in a way which led me to believe that it might be true. He pointed to the last hangar on the left. "That's our armament area. The next hangar up is where we have our mechanical shops … sheet metal, hydraulics, drag chute, and engine shop."

He turned to the right. "That last hangar is the electronics area … radar, autopilot, communications, and navigation … and that hangar there is the flight line area. Sergeant Townley's area is there too. My office is there, along with records, supply, and maintenance control. That's where we're going right now."

After what Major Bensen said about individual initiative versus trying to control people, I began to feel anxious to see maintenance control. At Chanute we learned maintenance control was the *brains* of maintenance, a centralized decision-making place, staffed with high ranking NCOs (Non Commissioned Officers) who planned, directed and controlled the maintenance work to insure efficiency.

Maintenance control did not always exist. In the early days of the Air Force, the responsibility for maintaining the aircraft rested with the flight line—the crew chiefs, flight chiefs, and the line chief. The idea for a centralized point of control evolved along with the growing complexity and sophistication of modern aircraft weapon systems. In maintenance school, our instructor assured the class that the next step in the process would be the utilization of computers 'to further increase efficiency and eliminate all human error'.

I followed Major Bensen through Hangar One and into a little room tucked in the back. It didn't surprise me to find maintenance control not the least bit impressive or highly staffed. A well-groomed staff sergeant sat facing a big, U-shaped metal console, which served as a mock-up of the entire squadron. Dark green paint represented the four maintenance hangars with the operations' building in the center painted yellow. The console sat directly in front of the sergeant who kept one hand on a mike as he surveyed the big board. To his left, a blue square filled with little magnetic model airplanes—the ones that took off earlier. An airman placed aircraft 380, the siphoning bird, in Hangar One, its destination. Another airman sat facing the console's right section where other smaller magnetic pieces indicated the location of all the ground support equipment in the squadron. The section on the left had a red cross-hatched area prominently labeled, ALERT BARN with tail numbered models 378, 375, 272, 260, and 251 inside the box.

Finally, the sergeant noticed the major and me in the back and jumped up. "I'm sure glad you came in, sir. I was about to get on the mike and call."

"Sergeant Conn, meet Lieutenant Joe Harrington, our new maintenance officer. Now, what's the problem, Sarge?"

We shook hands.

Appearing a bit nervous, the sergeant replied, "It's the colonel, sir. He called again this morning for a rundown on the birds."

"Is that so unusual?"

"No, sir, but I didn't know what to tell him about Three-sixty-three (363)," Sgt. Conn said, pointing at the little metal aircraft 363 on his board.

"Why didn't you just tell him that the flight line had work to do on the aircraft?"

"I told him that three days ago, sir. Remember when you said Townley wanted to look at the bird for awhile? Well, this is the third day that Townley has the aircraft. Yesterday, I was afraid the CO knew that it was really in commission, so I told him the crew chief couldn't find the forms. When he called again this morning, I didn't know what to say."

"Okay, I'll take care of it."

Sgt. Conn let out a sigh of relief and returned to the console.

Major Bensen turned to me. "Joe, I guess you're wondering what this is all about."

"Yes, sir."

"Come on, let's go over to my office and talk some before you get the idea we're playing games."

I followed the major's huge frame into the hall to another small narrow office, unimpressive by any stretch of the imagination. The sign on the door: MAJ. BENSEN—CHIEF OF MAINTENANCE.

The major squeezed between the wall and a big gray desk to get to a swivel chair. He reached into the knee pocket of his flight suit and pulled out his pipe and tobacco pouch. As he packed the pipe, I looked around and saw both walls covered with a collection of aircraft prints, most of which I could identify. I saw the twin-engine F-101 and the sleek F-102, both onetime primary ADC interceptors, but both retired to the deserts of Arizona or serving less strenuous duty with National Guard units. The old F-86 which became obsolete with the advent of modern weapon systems hung there along with the famous F-84 and the durable F-100, flown by the Thunderbirds. The major's desk was practically bare, except for one strange looking aircraft part shaped somewhat like a hubcap which served as an ashtray.

The pipe lit, Major Bensen raised one heavy flight boot onto the desk. "Now, getting back to Three-sixty-three (363). I wish the problem was only one bird, but I'm afraid it's more than that. Lately we've been seeing a lot of unusual things, like this morning when Three-eighty (380) siphoned fuel. I guess I don't have to tell you that an aircraft isn't supposed to dump fuel when it starts."

I nodded.

"Sergeant Townley tells me he's noticed an increase in other write-ups too ... like 'aircraft doesn't respond quickly' or 'controls seem sluggish'."

I asked, "Is it something serious?"

"Could be. Townley's been around airplanes a long time, Joe. You might say he has a sixth sense when it comes to that."

"And that's why he's taking a good look at Three-sixty-three (363), right?"

"Right, but I'm afraid after I see the colonel, we'll have to put it back on the flying schedule."

"Sergeant Townley didn't find anything then?"

"No. But in the case of the F-one-oh-six (F-106), it's not easy, Joe. Take the fuel system for example. There's a mess of valves ... check valves, float valves, fuel transfer valves, besides a complicated system of fuel lines."

"I see."

"Then there's another problem."

"What's that, sir?"

"The *Six* isn't in its prime anymore."

"I don't recall hearing about any accidents, sir. As a matter of fact, the way they talked in maintenance school, I thought it was a pretty reliable bird."

"That's true, but you have to understand something. You see, when an aircraft first comes into the inventory, there are a lot of problems and a lot of bugs to work out. That's the time you hear about accidents. Once you get through that phase, it's fine, until a bird starts getting old and wearing out. The Air Force never had an interceptor wear out on active duty, Joe, but I'm afraid that's what we're coming to with the F-one-oh-six (F-106)."

"Why is the Air Force letting it happen, sir?"

Major Bensen twitched his mustache. "Honestly, I'm not sure, but it's probably a lot of complicated reasons that I don't understand ... politics ... poor planning?"

"What about all the recent structural modifications made on the aircraft, sir? Won't that help?"

"I don't know," he replied. "Structural modifications are only external. None of the basic aircraft systems were improved, but a lot more weight was added."

The major glanced at his clock. "The first launch is down," he said, "and I have to see the colonel, remember? You can wait in the mess."

Chapter 2

Ground-pounders

The major went up to the colonel's office, and I helped myself to a cup of coffee. At the next table sat a young pilot, explaining his morning flight to several other pilots. The name on his flight suit, LT. TIM HOLT, the same pilot Sergeant Townley complained about earlier. He had straight black hair, sharp facial features and a cocky smile as he talked about his flight.

Listening to the conversation, I gathered that instead of the usual T-Bird intercept, a Navy F-4 had been in the area and vectored in as Lieutenant Holt's intercept, and after making a successful intercept, Holt and the Navy pilot had engaged in a little dogfight.

Holt beamed when he moved both hands to illustrate the battle. "The Navy jock zoomed up to fifty thousand feet with me right on his tail. He was a smart bugger. He went into a tight turn to shake me, thinking that I would turn to try to stay inside him."

The other pilots roared with laughter, and I thought I knew why. The F-106 had the reputation for not handling well in a tight turn. It could easily go into post-stall gyration and once in a stall or a spin, it would be hard to recover.

"Instead of turning, I pulled up, and I mean straight up, baby," Holt continued, as his right hand flew toward the ceiling. "Then I rolled back into the turn and dove down on his tail … ratta-tat-tat."

A victory roar erupted, and I smiled my congratulations.

About noon, Major Bensen came down from his meeting with the colonel, and looked anything but happy as we headed to the mess hall. An aroma of southern fried chicken permeated the mess and after contributing a dollar each, we took our place in line behind several pilots. After we seated ourselves, the other maintenance officers in the squadron joined us a short time later. Warrant Officer Wilbur Shock, slim and youthful-looking for a man of his rank, sat next to the major.

Major Bensen said, "Will is our whiz kid, Joe. He's in charge of the electronic shops."

Without any noticeable modesty, Will announced, "And that's why I'm the youngest warrant officer in the Air Force."

"That's right," the major confirmed.

Captain Frank Roberts, the Armament Officer, sat opposite me. Frank had straight brown hair and wore thick, horn-rimmed glasses. He seemed serious and quiet so I wondered if it had anything to do with him having responsibility for the squadron's nuclear arsenal.

The other maintenance officer, by far the most likable and outgoing, Captain Joseph Seimons had gray hair and immediately said, "Just call me Joe, Joe."

Captain Seimons supervised the mechanical shops, and as we ate our dessert, I noticed he wore pilot wings.

Major Bensen must have noticed my puzzled look and so he briefly explained. "Joe had an aircraft accident and came into maintenance."

"Oh, I'm sorry," I said, causing Warrant Officer Shock to break out in laughter and Captain Roberts to crack a weak smile.

The major said, "Not exactly an aircraft accident. You see—"

"Seimons interrupted, "Now, Major, wait a minute. I did have an aircraft accident, you know."

The remark made Warrant Officer Shock go into hysterics. Captain Roberts, back in his own world, continued eating his Jell-O.

"Since I'm such a jolly fellow," the captain explained, "I volunteered to play Santa Claus for the children's Christmas party last year. In the Fiftieth, Santa arrives by F-one-oh-six (F-106), and to make a long, embarrassing story short, I broke my leg climbing down the aircraft ladder."

With a big smile, Major Bensen said, "And then you learned what the real Air Force is all about."

"I won't deny I learned a thing or two," Captain Seimons admitted, also laughing. Then in dead seriousness he added, "And I'll always have a warm spot in my heart for maintenance."

"Joe will be back on flying status after the first of the year," the major explained.

Will quickly added, "Yeah, because it's easier."

"I won't deny that," Captain Seimons said, and we all laughed.

Before I left the mess to meet Master Sergeant Townley, Major Bensen instructed me to tell the sergeant that 363 would have to be *buttoned-up* and made ready for tomorrow's first flight and from his tone, I knew he didn't want to do it.

At one o'clock sharp, I waited in front of OPs (Operations) looking for Sergeant Townley. I saw the blue pickup parked in front of Hangar One, but no sign of the sergeant. After waiting ten more minutes, I decided to look in the flight line area and walked through Hangar One where several airmen worked on aircraft 380, and then went through a door into a big open area.

The flight line had a large open lounge. The crew chiefs had metal lockers which lined the wall separating the lounge from the hangar area and each of three F-106 flight chiefs had his own desk, labeled with his name and flight-A, B, and C. And a fourth, much smaller desk, belonged to Tech Sergeant Cummings, the T-Bird flight chief. Sergeant Townley had a little cubicle partitioned against one wall. A sign on the side read: CHIEF MASTER SERGEANT TOWNLEY-LINE CHIEF. At the next cubicle, clearly vacant and different only because it had a door with a sign on it that read—FLIGHT LINE MAINTENANCE OFFICER.

I heard the sergeant in his office, obviously chewing somebody out, so I walked away to a table covered with maintenance manuals.

Sergeant Townley spotted me, and I heard him say to the other person, "We'll talk about it later."

He came out of the cubicle. "Sorry to hold you up, Lieutenant. Come on, let's get out of here before I blow a gasket."

We drove along the apron, heading for the alert barn on the opposite side of the base and his silence prompted me to break the ice. "Problems, Sarge?"

"You said it, Lieutenant. It's this one airman named Buckley, and believe me, he can find more ways to screw off than a hamster in heat."

I laughed.

"No fooling, Lieutenant, the kid's something else. This morning, after I sent Hardy back to the barracks to change and get cleaned up, I told Buckley to take care of Hardy's bird when it got down. So the bird came down and Sergeant Grobly, he's the A-Flight chief, can't find Buckley. So I did a little checking and found out that he went on some base burial detail for Talifano."

"Base burial detail?"

"Yeah, some tech sergeant from base supply kicked the bucket and one of the pallbearers got sick," Townley explained.

"Maybe Buckley's just trying to be cooperative."

"Not a chance. Not Buckley … he's a goldbrick. Last week he pulled the same kind of stunt. Then, Talifano got him for the base litter detail. And I told him not to do anything for Talifano without his flight chief's permission. So what happens? He leaves a bird to go on a burial detail."

"I take it he's not a regular crew chief?"

Townley exclaimed, "Hell no! Every time we put him near an aircraft he pulls some disappearing act."

"Too bad. What are you going to do this time?"

"Probably nothing."

"Nothing?"

"That's right, Lieutenant … nothing. I've talked to Major Bensen several times about the situation, and he says we have to give the kid a chance to do his thing. Christ, I know what he likes to do best."

"What's that?"

"Like I said, Lieutenant … screw off."

"Well, what do you suppose the major has in mind?"

"Beats me," Townley replied. Then he paused for a few seconds and said, "He says that everybody has a need for something that satisfies himself."

"Yeah, I heard about that in college. I think they call it self-actualization."

"Oh yeah, Lieutenant," Townley said, sounding like he had a real revelation then added, "The last chief of maintenance I worked for would have told me to bust him."

"I've only been here half a day, and I can see Major Bensen has some different ideas."

Sergeant Townley chuckled. "Yeah, why do you think he's not a colonel at his age? Kind of strange for an ex-enlisted man, though."

"Oh … did he come up through the ranks?"

"Yeah … well, not exactly. He says he started in the old Army Air Corps as a pilot. The pilots were enlisted men then, you know."

"Yeah, I know."

"Then came the Air Force and he got into maintenance."

"So the major goes back to the Army Air Corps?"

"Yeah, me too," Townley said. "Boy, those were the days! I can remember when a young airman would fight for the chance to be a crew chief. Now, most of them want to get into electronics or armament … something fancy with more pay."

Sergeant Townley referred to specialists receiving additional pay, called pro-pay, as a special incentive the Air Force provided to attract and hold various technical specialists.

When we neared the far end of the apron, we came to a yellow warning stripe painted on the concrete so the sergeant stopped abruptly. "This is as far as we can go this way. An electronic eye protects the approach from the apron." Then pointing to a long, metal building in the distance, he said. "That's the alert barn there."

It looked like an all tin structure with six individual cells, three on each side of a taller structure, probably the living quarters for the pilots and airmen on duty.

The sergeant turned and followed the warning stripe off the apron and onto a base road. Soon, we came to a dirt road which led to a little guard shack at the entrance to the alert barn. I didn't have a security badge yet so we had to wait for fifteen minutes until the AP verified my clearance with operations.

Inside, the area seemed deserted except for several air policemen patrolling the perimeter with rifles. I followed Townley into the cell adjacent to the living quarters. Aircraft 251 stood on alert, looking monstrous in the enclosed cell. Instinctively, Townley started at the nose, where the spear-like pitot boom extended like a giant peashooter, and began checking the aircraft. I followed him back, past the air intake on the left side, to the landing gear wheel well.

I knew a nuclear tipped Genie rocket hung on the inside of the armament bay, and as we reached the tail section, Townley pointed to the polished afterburner section, saying, "There are still a few crew chiefs that take pride in their birds."

Only five minutes after entering the cell, a loud, staccato alarm sounded, sending a chill down my spine.

Townley looked amused and yelled, "I didn't plan this for your benefit, Lieutenant!"

A second later two crew chiefs ran into the cell. The first pressed a red button on the side wall. The front and rear doors slid up and over the aircraft. After the alarm stopped, a pilot rushed into the cell. By the time it took him to get in the cockpit the crew chiefs had the power connected and a mobile air compressor chugging away. The aircraft engine started with a whine. One crew chief yanked the chocks and the other ran to the front to direct the aircraft out. Quickly, 251 pulled out and headed for a runway. Then aircraft 272 raced out of the cell on the other side of the living quarters and followed 251.

When we returned to the squadron, we learned that a civilian airliner had entered our sector without proper identification.

Major Bensen's eyebrows twitched in a comical way as he said, "It could have been a Russian bomber."

At 1530, I followed Sergeant Townley to the electronics area in Hangar Two, and as Major Bensen suggested, I sat in on the NCO maintenance meeting, held every afternoon.

While we walked to the meeting, Sergeant Townley said, "The major might have some strange ideas, Lieutenant, but he's got some good ones, too."

"Oh? Like what?"

"Like this meeting we're going to. It gives everybody a chance to speak their peace and usually the work gets done right."

"Participation, huh?"

"Yeah, I guess you could call it that. If you ever want to see things get screwed up, just go to a squadron that goes by the book, where maintenance control dictates everything."

"Maybe someday I'll have the opportunity," I said as we entered the conference room.

Cigar smoke hung heavy in the little, confined space. Sergeant Conn from maintenance control sat at the head of a long narrow table with all the other seats occupied, except for one at the opposite end. Sergeant Townley introduced me to the other NCOs and took the empty chair.

I opened a metal folding chair and sat next to the wall as Sergeant Conn began the meeting. "Good afternoon, gentlemen, let's get started. We had twenty-five sorties scheduled today. We got in seventeen … not too good. The colonel is probably climbing all over Major Bensen right now."

Several of the NCOs chuckled and Sergeant Conn continued, "We have two night sorties scheduled for eight p.m.," then asked Sergeant Townley, "What birds can you give me?"

"Four-hundred (400) and Four-fifteen (415)," Townley replied.

Picking up a clipboard which had a single piece of paper with only the aircraft tail numbers scribbled in the left margin, Conn said, "Okay … then let's go through the other birds."

"The five birds standing alert have one more day to go before we have to rotate."

Looking to Townley again he asked, "How did Two-fifty-one (251) come back after the scramble this afternoon?"

Townley replied, "It's okay. The pilot wrote it up for nose wheel shimmy on the landing roll, but it's no wonder the way he turned on the way out. We tightened it up."

"Good," Conn said, making a note on his paper. "Next aircraft is Two-fifty-two (252). It flew two sorties today. First one it did all right, but after the second, the pilot wrote it up for 'nose wheel shimmy on takeoff roll … engine fire warning light comes on in flight with no sign of fire … and radar's out'."

Sergeant Tench, who represented the electronic shops, spoke up, "Let's pull Two-fifty-two (252) into Hangar Two first so we can get at that radar."

Sergeant Conn directed, "Okay, Two-fifty-two (252) goes to Hangar Two first—"

"Wait a minute." Townley interrupted then speaking to the other NCOs, he said, "You'd better let the flight line look at that shimmy first. We might need a high-speed taxi run to check it out. The shimmy probably caused the radar problem … it may have shook the hell out of it."

"Sounds reasonable," Conn said, looking to Sergeant Tench shifting in his chair.

"Well, yeah," said Tench then he explained, "but radar's been complaining they get a bird last and this means they get out late. Warrant Officer Shock instructed me to get radar going first."

Agreeing with Sergeant Townley, the other NCOs shook their heads in the negative. Several even gave a thumb-down signal to Sergeant Tench.

"That settles it then," Conn said. "Two-fifty-two (252) goes to the flight line first, and then we'll let the engine shop take a look at that fire warning."

Townley said, "The crew chief found the fire warning problem. He discovered a short between the pins in a disconnect. Corrosion caused it."

The NCOs then discussed the status and planned the work for the other aircraft. Aircraft 256 had an engine vibration and malfunctioning radar. The NCOs agreed that the engine shop would do their work first. Then the flight line would take the aircraft to the trim pad for a test run. Then the bird would be towed to Hangar Two where radar would do their work.

"We'll have Three-fifty-three (353) buttoned-up and ready for the morning flight," Townley said, following Major Bensen's directions and the colonel's orders to put it back in commission.

Conn exclaimed, "Thank heaven!"

"Don't be so thankful," said Townley. "We'll never find out what's causing our flight control problems unless I can have a bird for a week or two."

The NCOs laughed at Sergeant Townley's wishful thinking.

Sergeant Tench offered, "Maybe some of the pilots are blaming the birds when they miss their intercepts."

"I doubt that," Townley said. "Not that they're above such tactics," he added, again evoking some laughter.

Sergeant Conn said, "Well, we know you're not going to get a bird for a whole week, but if my recollection is correct, Two-eighty (280) goes to the depot in February or March for a complete tear-down inspection. Maybe they'll find the cause of the control problems then."

Sergeant Townley didn't say anything, but I could see by his expression that he didn't agree.

I learned that aircraft 380, which aborted on the early morning flight, dumped its fuel again when the engine started on the 1:30 launch. The flight line took the aircraft in order to check the fuel system. Aircraft 385 sat out of commission, waiting for two parts from supply, a fuel control assembly and a main gear actuator. Several days before, it had been grounded because of the fuel control assembly. When aircraft 400 developed a leak in one of its main gear actuators, 385 got cannibalized to put 400 back in commission then Major Bensen restricted further cannibalization. Sergeant Taft from squadron supply told the NCOs he would check with base supply as soon as the meeting ended. In the meantime, the NCOs decided to let aircraft 385 remain in Hangar Four with armament for nuclear load training.

Sergeant Conn closed the meeting with the next day's flying schedule. "Twelve aircraft at eight thirty, eight at ten thirty, and five at one thirty." And as the NCOs filed out he said, "Hold it, there's one more item I almost forgot. Sergeant Talifano called with a message from the colonel to remind all the troops that they must be in full, clean uniform at all times on the base."

One of the NCOs asked, "What if you live on base?"

All in all, it seemed like a very democratic meeting, with a lot of free discussion and some natural bickering. When differences arose, Sergeant Townley had the upper hand because he seemed to know more about the aircraft than the others. And when the meeting ended, Sergeant Conn certainly had the consensus needed to coordinate the work from maintenance control.

At the end of the day, Major Bensen asked me to join him for a quick drink at the officers' club. We arrived with the happy hour in full swing and pushed our way through a horde of pilots to a small table on one side of the long bar. Major Bensen waved and caught the attention of the waitress, a shapely brunette. She pushed and slid her way through the crowd, impervious to the admiring glances.

She drew a deep breath and asked, "What'll it be, Major?"

"Bourbon and water, Cindy."

She wrote it down and looked at me.

"A highball," I said, and she scrambled off.

For a brief moment the major focused his attention on the bar where Lieutenant Holt described his dogfight to a new group of pilots then he looked at me and said, "Well, Joe, tomorrow we put you to work."

"Good," I replied.

"As you saw today, there are a couple of slots open … flight line officer, and once Captain Seimons goes back to operations, the mechanical shops."

I nodded, giving my full attention. I knew about the officer slot open in maintenance control, but already I knew Major Bensen's feelings about control, and it didn't surprise me when he didn't mention that slot.

"But till you're ready for one of those jobs, Joe," he said, "I'd like you to spend some time in our records section."

"Fine, sir. When will I be ready for one of the other jobs?"

I guess my disappointment showed because the major leaned toward me and with a smile said, "Oh, don't worry about that, Joe, we'll both know. You'll be spending lots of time around airplanes. And since you're so eager, you can have the supply section too."

Our drinks arrived and for the next few minutes we talked about my first assignment in maintenance. All the while, the major kept an eye on Lieutenant Holt's group. And when their noisy conversation subsided somewhat, he waved and Holt came to the table.

"Joe, meet Tim Holt. Joe's our new maintenance officer."

Lieutenant Holt said, "Nice to meet you, Joe. Good luck."

"Thanks. Nice to meet you too, Tim."

Major Bensen said, "Heard about your flight today."

Holt said, "Yeah … what a battle, huh? That'll teach the Navy a little respect."

"The crew chief should get some of the credit," said the major. "He really got messed up climbing through the tailpipe."

Lieutenant Holt forced a weak laugh, but remained silent.

The major continued. "You remind me of a young pilot I once knew. He raised hell with the crew chiefs, too. Made them check over everything twice."

Holt crossed his arms then asked, "Oh yeah … what about it?"

"He crashed," the major said and I almost choked on my drink. Then he added, "Never did find out what happened."

Holt edged back to the bar, a telltale flush on his face.

Not very diplomatic, I thought, but the major kept his promise to Sergeant Townley.

We were about to call it a day when the Navy exchange pilot, Lieutenant Commander Thompson, pushed through the crowd and sat at our table. Well over six feet tall, with blond hair, and I guessed in his thirties, the commander now seemed younger than earlier on the flight line. Cindy appeared to be enamored by his presence.

Seeing Commander Thompson had shaved and showered, Major Bensen said, "I can see you didn't work up much of a sweat today."

Thompson laughed. "You're right, they had me scheduled in Three-eighty (380) all day. Thought maybe you'd have her ready for that one thirty go. No luck, huh?"

Major Bensen shook his head. "So far we found a few valves that look suspicious," he said, "but as long as we got her opened up we'll take a good look. The night shift will run her tonight," the major explained, crossing his fingers for luck.

Commander Thompson paused for a second then said, "A lot of pilots have been complaining about control problems."

"Yes, I know," Major Bensen said.

"I've noticed some sluggishness myself."

"The birds aren't spring chickens anymore, Buzz. We've been finding a lot of corrosion lately."

The commander gave us a solemn look. "That's too bad because it doesn't look like the Air Force is going to be getting any new aircraft for awhile."

"You sound like you know something."

"Yeah, well, if what I hear from some of my classmates in the Pentagon is true, I think you're stuck with the old One-oh-six (106) for some time to come."

Major Bensen leaned back, folding his arms across the open zipper of his flight suit.

Thompson continued, "The new Deputy of Defense wants competitive prototyping and fly-offs between the Navy and Air Force in order to select one aircraft to be used by both services. It's a big mess that started way back when the Defense Department told the Navy to develop the F-One-eleven (F-lll) and the Air Force to develop the F-Four (F-4). Well, the Navy didn't like having an aircraft shoved down its stack, so they torpedoed the program and went after the F-Fourteen (F-14)."

Then Major Bensen said, "And the Air Force had ideas of their own, I guess, and went after the F-Fifteen (F-15)."

"Right," Thompson agreed. "So now the Defense Department is trying to save money by selecting one aircraft for both services."

"And I thought the money went into missiles and submarines."

Commander Thompson laughed. "Well, that's part of it, too, I'm sure." Then changing the tone of the conversation the commander said, "What really bugs me ... is why the Air Force has such damn lousy officers' clubs? Just look at this place. Who's playing tonight? Oh, I remember. Ted Small and his Rhythm Masters. WOW! I hear the NCO club has a gorgeous stripper that goes all the way."

"I don't know about that," Major Bensen said, "but I've been in the service long enough to know why the Navy has nicer O-clubs and other recreational facilities."

"You do, huh? Okay, let's hear why."

Commander Thompson then leaned back to listen.

"Well, it's really quite simple. When the Navy gets money for a new air base, they build the O-club and other recreational facilities first. When the dough starts running out, it's time to put in runways.

Thompson groaned and sat upright, stopping the major from expounding any further.

As we got up to leave, Major Bensen said, "Well, if you don't believe me check on it someday."

In the parking lot, before we went our separate ways, Major Bensen said, "Joe, earlier you asked how we'll know when you're ready for more responsibility."

"Yes, sir."

"Well, there's a lot of ways of course, but getting invited to the NCO club is a pretty good indication. See you tomorrow."

That final comment made by Major Benson on my first day in the squadron, gave me something to think about after I got settled into the BOQ.

Chapter 3

Scarecrow One

The next morning, I began work in the records section with the official title of Officer in Charge of Records, Reports, and Analysis. Staff Sergeant Joseph Pardini, greeted me along with five busy airmen, including one short, black file clerk named Percy Williams, who seemed not the least bit affected by the others calling him *Little Sambo*. As Major Bensen promised, I also took charge of the squadron's two-man supply section, ably assisted by Technical Sergeant Elmer Taft, an experienced supply professional. The supply shop also had Airman Harold Rosenberg, a young talkative airman who hailed from New York City.

Immediately after shaking hands, Airman Rosenberg advised me that he liked to be called by his nickname—Rosy. Five minutes later Rosy made it a point to tell me his career plans didn't include the United States Air Force. He wanted to get a degree in political science by taking evening courses at Hyannis Community College and then find a job as a civilian for the government.

Both the records and supply offices had been conveniently located in Hangar One, right between maintenance control and Major Bensen's little office. Even though Major Bensen made it crystal clear to Pardini and Taft that my assignment would only be temporary, as I readied myself for one of the other maintenance jobs. Both NCOs seemed honored that an officer had been assigned to their sections.

Near the end of my first full week on the job, I overheard Sergeant Pardini talking to a visiting NCO from the engine shop. "Hey, guess what … I got myself an officer."

The NCO replied, "Well, make sure you keep him dry and feed him three times a day."

For several weeks, I kept myself busy in records, but I also became confused. The section operated like a beehive as squadron airmen and NCOs paraded through, seeking bits of information needed to complete their jobs. I read maintenance manuals, reviewed aircraft records and tried to familiarize myself with everything in the reports and files. A history of everything that ever took place in maintenance could be found there, but usually it took Sergeant Pardini to do the finding.

The amount of paperwork processed by the little section baffled me. Daily, a stack of directives arrived from ADC headquarters, requiring changes to the technical files and Air Force manuals. A constant barrage of maintenance reports requiring Major Bensen's signature left the office, and I noticed Sergeant Pardini made liberal use of the major's name stamp.

In supply section, the atmosphere might have been a little more subdued if not for the always effervescent Rosy who much preferred expounding on one of his political theories than completing a task assigned by Sergeant Taft.

Much to my chagrin, I discovered the difficulty in ordering even the smallest part for the F-106. In fact, it seemed to be a mind boggling task, demanding an intimate knowledge of the volumes of supply manuals, catalogs, and cross-reference indexes, which if stacked on end would surely reach the ceiling and form a wall across the room.

Rosy consoled me though, and after one frustrating attempt at ordering a part, he said, "Don't worry about it, Lieutenant, it's really more of an art than an exact science."

Sergeant Taft had the patience of a true supply professional and said, "It's very difficult to order a part for the *Six*, Lieutenant."

Rosy chirped in, "Yeah, because it's ancient."

Sergeant Taft explained. "It's like ordering something for a Model T Ford."

"Yeah, and the Air Force never buys anything from the same supplier more than once a fiscal year," Rosy said.

"Competitive bidding," I added.

"Yeah, that's it, Lieutenant," said Taft, "and to make matters worse the entire aerospace industry is in the doldrums."

To satisfy the stare from Sergeant Taft, Rosy said, "That's why I'm always reading *The New York Times* and *The Wall Street Journal* to find out who's going out of business."

One day Sergeant Taft left the office and Rosy confided in me. "The sad supply situation is happening because of Vietnam and not 'cause we supply arms to Israel."

He then added he wholeheartedly supported the latter cause.

Success finally came to me in supply. An item arrived that I alone researched and ordered—a box of thermocouples, heat sensing devices that Sergeant Singly from the engine shop needed.

Rosy found out I ordered the parts and became ecstatic. "Hey Sarge … get a load of this! The Lieutenant's order came in!"

"Great," Taft said, I think meaning to compliment me.

"Let's frame it like they do with the first dollar bill in a restaurant," Rosy suggested.

"I don't think Sergeant Singly would appreciate that," I said, ending the matter.

Major Bensen kept true to his promise and made sure that I didn't become overburdened with supply or record keeping duties. Each time I heard the *clump* of his flight boots approaching in the hallway (sounding somewhat like the charge of a bull elephant), I knew my salvation would be soon. He always walked in, greeting Sergeant Pardini and the airmen first. Then he came over and sat on the side of my desk, feet dangling as he lit the corncob pipe he liked so much.

He would say something like, "Radar has an interesting problem on Three-eighty (380) today," or "The hydraulic shop is repacking a cylinder in Hangar Three," or "The flight line is going to do a periodic inspection on Four-hundred (400) today."

He once presented me with a used flight suit and a pair of boots.

I didn't need the major's help to lure me out to the line for the spectacle of the morning preflights or the suspense and excitement of takeoffs and landings.

One cool morning, I watched from Hangar One as the first aircraft, 375 slowly began its take-off roll. The sound seemed to travel long distances on this day and the afterburner blast carried right into the hangar, reverberating against the tin walls and exposed steel beams. As the aircraft took off on runway 182, it startled me to see the base dump erupt with screaming gulls, many more than on that first day with Major Bensen.

The nose of the aircraft rose to penetrate the sky and as it flew over the end of the runway the pilot tried to escape the rising wall of gulls, but unable to avoid contact, the aircraft penetrated the edge of the solid white curtain. The engine paused then resumed again with a sputter. The pilot made an abrupt turn, heading 375 back to the approach end of the runway. My view partially blocked by the hangar, I stood frozen, watching what I could as the struggling aircraft flew dangerously low over the base.

Both the meat wagon (ambulance) and fire trucks screamed onto the runway and 375 reappeared, turning short and low onto final approach. The aircraft made it to the edge of the runway, and a moment later the pilot set it down very hard.

I waited until Sergeant Townley delivered the shaken pilot in the rear of his pickup. Major Harmon, the chubby operations officer, hopped off the back, leaving his gear and hurried toward operations. His orange flight suit looked all wet except for the few dry spots at the elbows and knees.

It took the better part of the day for Sergeant Singly and several airmen from the engine shop to remove the power plant and assess the damage. The compressor section looked severely damaged with feathers, bones, and guts plastered throughout.

I thought, *What a ghastly sight.*

The next morning I sat with Major Bensen in the pilots' lounge as he waited for Colonel Wyler to meet with the base commander, General Braddock, to once again discuss the relocation of the base dump. The major fiddled with his tight fitting collar.

After seeing him in only an orange flight suit and boots, he looked unnatural in his dress blues and he confessed the colonel insisted he wear the uniform for their meeting. He also revealed he wanted to have the flight line tow the sickly looking engine over to base headquarters, but the colonel considered the idea too theatrical.

They returned from the meeting before the first flight landed. General Braddock had decided to establish a committee to study the dump's relocation.

With a disdain befitting the plague, Major Bensen blurted out, "A committee!"

I said, "I take it you don't like committees."

"It's not that I don't like them," the major said, "it's just that they're indecisive. It's the best way of blurring responsibility."

"In maintenance school they said committees were good for creating new ideas."

"Did they tell you that they're also self perpetuating?"

"No."

Pending a solution, the squadron had the mission of clearing out the gulls before the first aircraft took off on runway 182.

The colonel decided the job belonged to maintenance and Major Bensen assigned the job to Sergeant Townley, who growled, "What do dumps and seagulls have to do with fixing airplanes?"

Young Airman Buckley volunteered to handle the gull detail whenever the wind blew such that the aircraft flew runway 182.

At Major Bensen's suggestion, I made the trip to the dump with Airman Buckley one morning prior to launch. Buckley, a tall, skinny kid with a baby face and a mop of unruly dark hair, drove like a demon for the dump. On the way, he opened up to me and seemed very friendly, admitting he found a home in the Air Force just as the recruiter promised.

At the end of the pavement, he continued off onto a narrow dirt road without slowing down until we reached the dump. He set the brake and called, "Control, this is Scarecrow One … all set."

After a pause Sergeant Conn replied, "Roger, Scarecrow One, stand by till I call operations."

Buckley surprised me and took a loaded .45 Colt pistol from a holster lodged between the seats.

I asked, "Who keeps the gun?"

"Sergeant Conn keeps it locked in the safe in maintenance control. I completed firearms training and all the safety stuff," he added, putting me a little more at ease.

"Scarecrow One, this is Control. Okay, get rid of them seagulls."

"Roger, Control," Buckley said with authority.

He inserted ear plugs, added ear muffs and hopped out of the truck. I noticed his fatigues, oversized except for the length of the trousers which looked ready for high water. He aimed the gun over the dump and fired six quick resounding blasts. The dump exploded with the cries and squeals of the protesting birds. With the last gull departing, Buckley hopped into the truck and confirmed to control his accomplishment. Just as we started back the first aircraft roared like thunder over our heads.

I asked, "Any chance of them coming back today?"

He appeared proud of his contribution and stated with certainty, "No, sir … maybe a few stragglers, but nothing to worry about."

"Are some mornings more hectic than others?"

"Yes, sir. I think I got it figured out though. It depends on what they serve in the base mess. Mondays on the dump are real bad because the base usually has seafood on Friday and they bring everything over on the weekend. I've been keeping a little record."

He showed me his little black notebook which indicated the activity at the dump and a lot of other interesting facts, such as weather conditions, wind velocities, and of course the daily servings at each of the mess halls on base.

Sergeant Townley waited near the open hangar as we arrived back and as soon as Buckley went on his way, Townley asked, "Well, Lieutenant, what do you think … self-actualization, huh?"

"I don't think it's exactly what Major Bensen has in mind, but it seems like a good start."

Sergeant Townley looked a little disappointed, but still managed a husky laugh and headed toward Hangar Three.

In late November the bright red skies of Indian summer faded and the days became noticeably cooler. The pilots, knowing that the colder air meant more thrust from the Dart's engine, approached the aircraft with renewed enthusiasm. Sergeant Taft used his influence with a buddy in base supply and presented me a warm, flight jacket to wear over my orange flight suit.

Major Bensen seemed to ignore the nip in the air except on the really cold mornings when I saw he wore woolen underwear. The major appeared to be forever on the move, observing the work, listening to what the men had to say, and always providing some word of encouragement before moving along. Rosy said the major took the pulse of maintenance.

Master Sergeant Talifano, the first sergeant, also made himself a familiar sight in maintenance. He frequently wandered about the hangars and the flight line, always dressed in his immaculate blue uniform and quickly pounced on any airman out of uniform or unfortunate enough to accumulate an excessive amount of oil, grease, or fuel on his fatigues; to the first sergeant, the word excessive seemed to mean noticeable. Only Airman Buckley, his eager volunteer, got a pass from being scrutinized.

All the other airmen fell prey to the feared first sergeant except those working close to Sergeant Townley. The line chief made it clear he regarded Talifano's vigilance an unnecessary intrusion upon the progress of maintenance.

The situation prompted Warrant Officer Shock to remark, "Townley and Talifano remind me of like poles of a magnet."

Without giving his comment any thought, I asked, "Why's that?"

Will looked at me as if to suspect my technical knowledge and said, "Because they repel each other, of course."

Since reporting in, I only got upstairs in the operations building one time to pick up my security badge. But I did get to see Janice quite often because she usually arrived about the time we finished breakfast in the mess. Once she stopped in the hall and asked about maintenance, and I noticed her deep blue eyes.

Chapter 4

Nukes for Christmas

As a new maintenance officer, one of my assignments involved becoming qualified as a nuclear loading officer and Captain Roberts needed to train me for that awesome responsibility. Every day that I reported to Captain Roberts in Hangar Four, he remained as mysterious as the first day we met. Each time I entered the hangar and headed for his glass cubicle at the rear, he shoved all his papers and memos back into his desk drawer. I got the distinct feeling that we might be in different Air Forces so I mentioned the matter to Major Bensen.

"Don't feel bad," the major said. "I'm not allowed to see any of that stuff either … unless there's a need to know for maintenance."

Each session with Captain Roberts went the same. Without a word spoken, I would follow him underneath an aircraft sitting in the hangar for load training. We both sat on the same side of the armament bay and observed as the armament technicians loaded then unloaded dummy nuclear tipped Genie rockets. Capt. Roberts sat with a stopwatch and a clipboard, timing the load and noting any discrepancies while I followed the procedures on a checklist. After each load the captain gave a critique, and the next team moved in.

After a month of watching—Captain Roberts never let me touch anything but the checklist—Colonel Wyler called for a *Sunday Punch*, the squadron code name for a live nuclear load. It came at four in the morning, and I rushed out to the line where twelve aircraft sat waiting in groups of four. Captain Roberts assigned me to the middle group and positioned me where I could see all the activity around all four aircraft. Warrant Officer Shock had the group on my left and Captain Seimons the group on my right.

After each aircraft had a crew chief and an armament loading team in place, the base air police roped off the entire area. Then a convoy of four tractors, each towing four nuclear weapons' trailers connected end-to-end, emerged from one corner of the munitions building located in the woods behind Hangar Four. The convoy moved slowly, led by an AP truck with a red, flashing light. Each weapon had a canvas cover and rested on a little yellow trailer marked DANGER on every side. The convoy proceeded behind the line of aircraft; a nuclear Genie got deposited at each aircraft and placed in a specially marked spot on the side of the armament bay. The armament teams removed the covers carefully and inspected the weapons.

My responsibility during the weapons load involved watching from a distance. If all went well, I had nothing to do, but if a problem arose—with a weapon or the aircraft—I had to decide to continue or to stop the load. Captain Roberts instructed me to "do whatever the loading chief recommends".

As luck would have it, a problem developed on my very first load. During the loading of my four aircraft, 301 began siphoning fuel near the armament bay. With a Genie already hung in the opened bay, the technicians began to button up and saw the fuel. They immediately backed away and signaled me. I rushed to the aircraft while the crew chief ran underneath to try to stop the siphon.

He yelled to one of the armament technicians, "Cut the power!"

The technician looked confused and ran in circles for a moment then made a mistake, going for the refueling receptacle instead of the power cable.

The crew chief hollered, "No! That's the wrong one!"

Too late.

The technician yanked the fuel nozzle from the aircraft and fuel began to inundate the entire area. The crew chief directed one of the other armament technicians, a tall skinny airman, to get a fire extinguisher, but in going around the nose of the aircraft the armament technician forgot about the aircraft pitot tube sticking out in front and *zap*, down he went, cut down at the neck.

We soon had things under control and someone took the airman to the hospital. I found out later he was okay but embarrassed.

To complete my training, Captain Roberts agreed to let me see the munitions site secluded in the wooded area about a quarter mile off the apron. It reminded me of the morgue I visited on a class trip in high school. The nuclear weapons rested (under strict temperature and humidity conditions) in casket-like containers in separate vaults. At the captain's directions, a somber looking staff sergeant unlocked one of the many heavy metal doors and slid a weapon out for viewing. Except for it being all white (the dummies carried on the aircraft during the daily flying had red nose sections), it looked identical in every respect.

Thank God everyone wasn't as spooky as Captain Roberts. Warrant Officer Shock always tried to teach me something about his specialty, electronics, only he couldn't understand why I didn't grasp everything as quickly as he thought I should. Captain Seimons seemed always so friendly and ready to lend a helping hand. I noticed the captain spent a lot of time in the flight trainer, getting ready to transition back to flight status. The official time for his transfer back to operations would be the instant he *safely* reached the bottom of the ladder during the children's Christmas party, and from my contact with him, I sensed he looked forward to that with mixed emotions. I could only guess that maybe maintenance had gotten into his blood a little.

I liked Captain Seimons and we often talked about maintenance or just shot the breeze. Of all the maintenance officers, I depended upon him if I had a problem or needed information about the F-106.

One cold, blustery day in the middle of December, it struck me sitting in supply that I had been in the squadron quite a while, and I still didn't know how the old Dart accomplished an intercept. It really didn't matter a lot if a maintenance officer didn't know all the specifics, but it still bothered me because I had the creeping suspicion that any day Rosy would ask me to explain such a *simple* thing as the intercept.

So I walked out of supply and onto the wind-blown apron then headed to Hangar Three. A light snow had fallen the night before, and the flakes danced and swirled as I walked past operations to the mechanical shops area. The hangar door stood open. I turned into the protection of the hangar, spotting Captain Seimons, sleeves rolled up and working with Sergeant Singly and another airman on the removed engine of aircraft 378.

As I approached, Captain Seimons exclaimed, "Hey! Here comes our supply officer with some good news."

I saw his hands covered with grease from the elbows down as I announced, "Nothing came in today."

Sergeant Singly said, “Maybe tomorrow.”

Captain Seimons asked, “What can we do for you, Joe?”

“There’s something I wanted to ask you,” I replied, “but I see you’re pretty busy. Maybe I can come back later.”

“Not a chance. If there’s something on your mind, we’ll talk about it now. Come on, let me get cleaned up first,” he said then I followed him to the sink. While scrubbing his hands, he continued, “I notice you spending time on the line with Sergeant Townley.”

“Yeah, Major Bensen thought it would be a good idea.”

“It sure is. Townley’s the guy to stay close to if you want to learn about maintenance and airplanes.”

“Yeah, major said he has a sixth sense about airplanes.”

“I believe that,” said Captain Seimons, wiping his hands. “I haven’t been around maintenance for too long, but I think the major has that sixth sense, too.”

“About airplanes?”

I noticed what I thought might have been a sly, disarming smile as he answered, “No, about people.”

I told Captain Seimons the reason I came over then he directed me to the nearest aircraft in the hangar and up into the cockpit.

“It’s all very simple,” he said, standing on the ladder, looking into the cockpit. As I sat back, nervous and confused by the maze of indicators and instruments, he continued, “All the work is done on the ground, and a clever monkey could make a good intercept.”

I laughed and felt more relaxed.

“I’m serious,” he insisted then went on to explain: “A ground-based radar controller identifies the target on his radar scope and aims a light gun at the blip. Then, a ground-based computer figures out the target’s speed, distance and direction of flight. With this information, another ground-based computer works out an intercept path and automatically feeds the information to the *Six* with a silent UHF data link. The information is presented right there,” he said, pointing to a display between my legs. “It tells the pilot which direction to fly and how fast to get there. Actually, if he wants to, the pilot can turn on the autopilot … and the autopilot takes the information and flies the bird to the intercept point.”

“Yeah, it is pretty simple,” I agreed.

"I told you so. Now, once he's at the intercept point, all the pilot has to do, if he's still awake, is push that little button there to lock onto the target and arm the weapons, which will fire automatically at the right time. Once fired, the Falcon missiles have their own guidance system."

"I see … and if the target is a whole formation, you fire the nuclear Genie."

"Right … just let it go and get the hell out."

"What about the radar on the aircraft?"

"Good question. The radar on the *Six* is good, but it has a short range. The pilots let the ground radar do the work until they get close to a target. Then they exercise the radar on board to make sure it works okay in case the ground stations ever get knocked out."

Each year, according to custom, the annual squadron children's Christmas party takes place on the Saturday before Christmas. On a crisp, windy day I arrived at Hangar One an hour before the scheduled arrival of Santa Claus. The closed hangar bustled with excitement and activity. The children made a lot of noise in a special section of tables set up just for them, horseshoe fashion, in the center of the hangar and decorated with colorful place settings and piled with lots of goodies to eat and drink. At the open end of the horseshoe a raised platform would be Santa's stage to dispense the gifts. A giant Christmas tree, decorated with large red balls, stood in the center of the horseshoe table arangement.

Master Sergeant Talifano had been in charge of the preparations during the week, and with the help of Airman Buckley and a host of crew chiefs, all remnants of aircraft maintenance had been removed from the usually cluttered flight line hangar. It took a strong solution of muriatic acid to remove all the grease and grime from the floor. Then it got several coats of wax. The floor looked brilliant and sparkled with the reflection of the Christmas tree lights. Beautiful pine cone wreaths adorned the hangar walls and strings of holly and mistletoe hung from the rafters.

It had all been accomplished while Sergeant Townley muttered, "Why is Hangar One always the squadron's ceremonial hangar?"

While Airman Buckley and several other airmen catered to the children, the other squadron members, their wives and families, congregated in separate groups around the inside perimeter of the hangar. The affair seemed more than just a party for the children; it seemed more like an annual social event where acquaintances got renewed and friendships rekindled. It did seem strange seeing everyone in civilian attire and on more than one occasion, I had difficulty placing people where they worked in the squadron.

As a bachelor, I roamed from group to group, meeting many of the families. Major Bensen sat with his wife, Margaret, in a group with the other maintenance officers and some pilots, including Major Harmon and his chubby wife, Hilda, Captain Johnson, the squadron's public information officer and his wife and Captain Lickle, a short nervous type, the squadron's flight safety officer with his much taller wife.

I met Mabel Seimons, a charming woman, and her daughter and son-in-law and their two five-year-old twin girls. The girls kept asking, "Where's Grandpa?"

"Grandpa had to go flying," Mrs. Seimons kept repeating. "He'll be here soon," she promised.

The electronic technicians sat in the right upper corner of the hangar and Warrant Officer Shock and his pretty, red-haired wife, Isabel, seemed to be the center of attention there. The airmen from the flight line had their own group, as well as the airmen from the mechanical shops. Most of the NCOs sat together near the left front.

About quarter to one, Colonel Wyler and General Braddock, both in dress blues, arrived with their wives. The general looked impressive—tall and statuesque as you would expect a general to look. They wandered from group to group, meeting the airmen and their families while offering their best holiday wishes.

At exactly one o'clock, someone in the NCO group called for silence. When the rumble of voices died, I detected the whine of a jet engine. "It's Santa Claus," an NCO announced from the set up stage. "Open the doors," he ordered and several airmen rushed to open the big, sliding doors.

The F-106, still far out on the taxiway, moved straight for the hangar. Airman Buckley and several others did their best with a restraining rope to hold back the children and everyone crowded near the entrance. Aircraft 415, one of the two aircraft in the squadron with dual cockpits, moved closer with its canopy up. The pilot in the front seat wore a deer rack fastened to his helmet. Someone said that Lieutenant Parks, my next door neighbor in the BOQ, and also the youngest pilot in the squadron, had the honor, by custom, of escorting Santa from the North Pole (the alert barn) to the squadron. When the aircraft got close enough, the crew chief signaled Parks to turn, exposing Santa in the rear seat to the delight of the screaming children.

When the pilot cut the engine, Buckley dropped his end of the rope and the children ran screaming to the aircraft. Captain Seimons played the role to perfection, waving and shouting, "Ho Ho's" from the rear cockpit. Lieutenant Parks sat with a big, proud smile. Someone placed a ladder on 415 and protected it from the grasps of excited children. Captain Seimons carefully struggled down with his big bag of presents, finally jumping the last several feet to the concrete. A loud cheer arose from the hangar entrance and Captain Seimons, jolly as ever, led the mob of happy tots back to the hangar.

With everyone seated again, Santa called each child up to the platform and presented a gift along with a kiss or a handshake.

As Captain Seimons was about to jump off the platform, Major Bensen stepped up, carrying a big burlap bag. "And now, Santa, I'd like to give you a gift from everyone in maintenance," the major announced, reaching into his bag and pulling out a set of aircraft chocks, beautifully plated with shiny aluminum aircraft panels. Pointing to the inscription engraved on one of the chocks, the major asked, "Would you please read?"

"Sure," said Captain Seimons. "From Maintenance … Once a Ground-pounder—" Choking up, he wiped a tear from his face and went on. "Always a Ground-pounder," then he jumped off the platform.

The applause was deafening.

Ask any serviceman who has ever spent a holiday on a stateside military base while almost everyone else goes home and he will tell you about the loneliness. There are no USO shows or Bob Hope extravaganzas, complete with beautiful girls, to alleviate the low-down feeling. Such was my plight during Christmas week since I had used up all my allotted leave after flight training. I only felt sorry for myself a short time because I thought about our troops in Vietnam and their big sacrifice. *How many would trade places?* The obvious answer made me ashamed.

December had been a good month for flying and we scheduled only a few sorties a day in Christmas week. The other maintenance officers all took leave and only Major Bensen faithfully stopped in each day. In the latter part of the week Colonel Wyler and Major Harmon flew to ADC headquarters in Colorado Springs for some important operations meeting.

On Christmas Eve, after a lone sortie early in the morning, the squadron seemed really dead. I wandered around the hangars for awhile then went to the pilots' mess. As a thoughtful gesture, the cook left some coffee brewing. As I poured a cup, I heard typing coming from the second floor so I carried my cup up the stairs.

Janice's radiant smile immediately dispelled a lot of my gloom and self pity. I think she understood how I felt because she stopped typing and we talked for some time about the usual things, such as families, hobbies, our backgrounds and ambitions.

She lived with her parents and six-year-old brother Mark in North Falmouth, a little village a few miles from the base. I learned she was a native, born and raised on Cape Cod and attended college for a year before taking a job in the squadron. Her father, an ex-Army sergeant, and the business manager for a local cranberry plant, received his discharge at Olefield and decided to settle on the Cape.

Janice invited me to dinner on Christmas Day so I accepted. The family seemed warm and happy and her mother treated me extra special, like a long lost son. We enjoyed a sumptuous turkey dinner with lots of cranberry sauce of course, and then sat around the fireplace in their cozy Cape Cod home. While little Mark kept busy with all his new toys, Janice proudly displayed some of her oil paintings and sketches of the local landscape. Quite to my embarrassment, the Jablonski family even presented me with a Christmas present, a beautiful sweater.

Janice's father seemed very interested in the squadron and we talked for some time about my work as a maintenance officer.

As I left, I mentioned it to Janice then she laughed and said, "Oh, he just wanted to make sure you're not a pilot."

Chapter 5
Winter Woes

We began the New Year with a commander's briefing in the pilots' conference room on the first floor of Ops. By lining the walls three deep, the entire squadron, about 150 personnel squeezed into the room and as we waited, I could only envy the happy faces of those who spent the holiday with family and friends. Major Harmon waited at the door and when the colonel started down the staircase steps, he called out, "Squaaa … dron, ahh … tennn … shun!"

The CO walked with a brisk pace to the raised platform in front of the crowded room then ordered, "Be seated, gentlemen. I know it's crowded in here so I plan to keep this short. First off, let me say I can see by all the happy faces that you're glad to be back at the fighting 50th."

A cheerful rumble passed through the room.

"I want to tell you," the colonel continued, "how proud I am of the excellent team we have here at the 50th. We don't always get the recognition that some of our sister commands receive, but as true professionals, I know you're aware of the contribution each of you is making to our country's security."

The colonel went on for another half hour, talking about the war in Vietnam and how the public attitude toward the military had changed and how we all needed to show strength in ADC in order to convince our enemies that it would be *pure folly* to even consider any aggressive act.

Finally, he came to what everyone waited to hear, the proposed flying schedule. "You've all heard that our flying requirements will be increased. Well, I hope I've explained why." The colonel paused deliberately, took a deep breath then continued, "So for the first quarter of the new year, our quota will be fifteen hundred sorties and two thousand hours. I know that's quite an increase, but with everyone's cooperation …" He paused again and looked at Major

Bensen who sat next to me fooling with his pipe then said, "I'm sure we'll surpass our goal."

The room stayed dead silent. Everyone looked sullen.

"Now, there's only one final item," the colonel said. "ADC headquarters has given me their word that we won't have an Operational Readiness Inspection until we go through the Weapons School at Tyndall Air Force Base, Florida."

Someone yelled out from the rear, "Look out for the ORI next week," and the room exploded with laughter, followed by a cheer for the outspoken airman who stood and took a bow.

Colonel Wyler shuffled his feet on the platform and said, "Well, they promised anyway. We're scheduled to go down to Tyndall at the beginning of the summer."

Finished, he hopped off the platform. Everyone stood up and waited in place as he made his way out.

When the colonel came to Major Bensen, he asked without stopping, "Think the radars will hold up, Major?"

"Radars don't fly, Colonel … airplanes do," the major quipped and the colonel continued out the door without responding.

For the first several weeks in January, the aircraft performed great, probably like they did in their prime. The weather stayed good and Sergeant Conn's status board indicated good progress toward the goal with both sorties and flying hours well ahead of schedule. Then a northeaster hit and brought a ton of snow, and it took several days to dig out. Janice said that a storm like that came every once in a while to remind the Cape natives of their New England heritage.

On the first flying day after the storm, the wind blew fierce and the temperature went down to a bitter 10° F. I made my way through the drifts and joined Sergeant Townley on the line just as the pilots began their preflights. Twelve aircraft sat on their spots, and Colonel Wyler in 400 encountered a problem first. The crew chief signaled Townley, and he drove up behind the aircraft.

We jumped out and Townley asked, "What's up, Clymer?"

The young airman stood with his hands on his hips and head down. "The colonel found some hydraulic fluid leaking from the left gear, Sarge."

Townley saw the colonel had already removed his gear and we both knew he couldn't save the flight. Besides, the crew chief of 272 on the next spot waved to us because he also had some sort of a problem. I followed the sergeant over and under the wing of 272. The airman frantically wiped an actuator on the main gear.

Lieutenant Parks watched as he said, "If he can stop that actuator from leaking, Sarge, I'll take the bird."

The crew chief said, "No way, Sarge," squeezing more hydraulic fluid from the rag.

As I looked down the line there appeared to be more serious discussions taking place.

I followed Sergeant Townley back to the pickup and as soon as we jumped in, Control called: "Flight line one, come in."

Townley answered, "Go ahead, Control."

Sergeant Conn asked, "What's going on out there?"

"We got a few leaking cylinders."

"How many aircraft are out?"

"So far it looks like four or five. No, wait … looks like Major Harmon has a problem too. I better get down there."

"Okay," Sergeant Conn said, "but let me know as soon as possible … out."

By the time we reached Major Harmon's bird, the crew chief had stopped the hydraulic leaks. Townley smiled and gave the young airman a pat on the back. Major Harmon climbed back into the cockpit and a minute later started the engine. Townley and I jumped back into the truck, but before we moved, fuel began to siphon from under the aircraft. The young crew chief acted quickly and ran under the aircraft. He almost put his lips on the cold aircraft, over a vent hole, to blow in to try and stop the siphon.

Townley yelled in time, "No! Your lips will stick!"

The crew chief backed away for a moment, cupped his hands and blew into the vent, stopping the siphon.

Major Harmon started the engine again but once again the fuel poured out. The major cut the engine and aborted the flight.

By the time we reached aircraft 381, Lieutenant Commander Buzz Thompson had already aborted for leaks.

Captain Seimons, anxious to fly after a year in maintenance, accepted aircraft 378, satisfied that the nose gear cylinder had stopped leaking, but when he started the bird, the fuel started to siphon. After two more unsuccessful tries, Captain Seimons aborted his flight also.

Of all the aborted flights, one really got to Sergeant Townley. The crew chief waved from aircraft 375 and we rushed over to it. Captain Lickle, the squadron's flight safety officer, began walking away with his gear.

Townley asked the crew chief, "What's the problem?"

The crew chief declared, "Nothing, Sarge! The captain says the bird's leaking hydraulic fluid, but it's not … anywhere."

Townley called out, "Captain!"

Captain Lickle turned around momentarily then waved Townley away and continued on his way to Operations.

Coming back to the truck fuming, Townley huffed,. "There's one pilot who's afraid of his own shadow. That's why they made him the flight safety officer … keeps him on the ground a lot. Christ … the other day he almost landed with the gear up."

"Oh yeah, what happened?"

"He just forgot to put the gear down. Lucky the mobile caught it in time. They shot flares at the last instant."

Only one aircraft got off the ground that bitter cold morning. Six aborted for leaking hydraulic cylinders and five for fuel siphoning. The rest of the day didn't get any better. Sergeant Townley called it the worst day he ever experienced on the line.

In the next several weeks, the flight line and hydraulic shop worked countless hours of overtime, replacing seals and repacking cylinders until finally the hydraulic leaks stopped. As insurance, Major Bensen took Sergeant Townley's advice and had the heat in the hangars turned down so the aircraft wouldn't suffer temperature shock when pulled out to the line.

The fuel siphoning problems continued and became worse until almost every aircraft dumped fuel upon start up. Even though Sergeant Townley warned all the crew chiefs about putting their lips on the cold aircraft metal, one young airman did it anyway. He became stuck until another airman yanked him free, leaving his lip skin still glued to the aircraft. Thereafter, Townley provided each crew chief with a small, rubber hose they carried under their belts at all times.

Hoping to fix the fuel system problems, Major Bensen requested assistance from the depot. But the depot wanted us to fly an aircraft out to them so we called the aircraft manufacturer. The next day, a fuel systems engineer from the manufacturer arrived and with colorful charts and diagrams eloquently explained the intricate workings of the fuel transfer scheme. However, confronted with a real siphoning aircraft, the engineer couldn't pinpoint the specific valve or mechanism causing the malfunction. Dejected, he left the next morning, promising to call as soon as he had an answer. As far as I know, we never heard from him again.

Janice and I began dating a lot by then, and she enjoyed keeping me informed of the colonel's efforts to put pressure on Major Bensen to find a solution to the fuel problems. She said each time the colonel confronted Major Bensen, the major tried to explain the intricacies of the fuel system and the fact that each aircraft operated a little different.

She said one time, the colonel slammed his fist on the desk after listening to Major Bensen and gave the major an ultimatum, saying the colonel screamed he didn't want any more excuses, just an end to the siphoning or else. She said the outburst shocked her and even Sergeant Talifano stuck his head out of his office and looked concerned.

We never did find out what the or else meant because fortunately for Major Bensen, and I guess the whole squadron, one of the airmen on the flight line came up with a simple, but ingenious, idea for troubleshooting the fuel system. Sergeant Townley, along with several airmen, fabricated a set of transparent tubes, identical in size and shape to the fuel lines on the aircraft.

One at a time, the aircraft were outfitted with "the flight line's contraption," as Warrant Officer Shock called it, and you could actually see the fuel as it transferred from tank to tank through the system. When siphoning occurred, the obstruction, usually a sticking check valve or malfunctioning float valve, could be seen and immediately repaired.

With the fuel leaks finally under control, we began to make headway toward meeting the flying schedule. But an unexpected kind of leak occurred which caused almost as much disruption.

Sergeant Townley and I watched from the pickup as the last aircraft of the afternoon launch taxied out. The sergeant turned the pickup toward the hangar and Airman Bean waved at us as he walked toward the truck. He held a set of wet aircraft forms in two fingers and at arm's length like holding a dead rat by the tail.

Bean said, "Look what one of them eggheads did, Sarge."

Looking at the soggy forms, Townley asked, "Fuel?"

"Heck, no, Sarge. That idiot Hardesty used the pilot's relief-tube on the transient bird from South Carolina."

"Okay, Bean, settle down and tell me exactly what happened."

"Well, when the bird came in, Sergeant Grobly told me to service it. Everything was all right except for the intercom. So I waited out there, trying to keep warm until Communications got there to fix it. Finally, this jerk Hardesty, comes and starts working in the cockpit. Last week he left orange peels in a cockpit and—"

Growing impatient, Townley asked, "Never mind last week, Bean, what happened now?"

"Well, in that aircraft the pilot's relief tube dumps out right at the nose wheel and I put the forms there, under a tire so they wouldn't blow away."

The veins in Townley's neck throbbed and his face turned a shade of purple then looking Bean straight in the eyes he said, "Well, what are you doing with the forms? Why didn't you get him to make out a new set?"

"I tried, Sarge, but he refused. He said it was my job. And it's a big job to write up all new forms and—"

Townley screamed, "Your job? Bean, what the hell kind of crew chief are you?" Airman Bean dropped his eyes and Townley continued, "You're responsible for that bird and everything that happens on it. Now get the hell out there and make Hardesty straighten out that mess."

Airman Bean headed for the electronics hangar still holding the forms out as far as his arm could reach.

With an apparent change of heart, Townley called out, "Bean, wait a minute. Come back here. Listen … forget what I said, okay? I'll take care of it."

"Sure, Sarge."

"Throw those forms in the back of my truck. I'll take care of this one myself. Those pro-pay bastards have gone too far this time," he declared then we drove off.

Fortunately, the grapevine in the squadron is quite efficient, and Major Bensen, accustomed to being tuned in, interceded just as Townley and Warrant Officer Shock stood eyeball to eyeball, separated only by the smelly forms of the transient aircraft.

Will Shock argued, "When you gotta go, you gotta go. Besides, the forms are the crew chief's responsibility."

After due consideration and much to Townley's satisfaction, Major Bensen instructed Will to have Hardesty redo the forms.

That afternoon, as Sergeant Pardini and I updated some technical manuals, a dejected Airman Hardesty walked in and asked if we had blank aircraft forms. We had a new set of forms already waiting on the counter so he grabbed them and left.

Later at the O-club, Major Bensen told me why he decided in favor of Sergeant Townley and the flight line, beginning like the classic fairy tale, "Once upon a time, a crew chief ruled supreme over his aircraft and everything had to be done to his satisfaction."

"Not anymore, huh?"

"Unfortunately not. It's difficult for a crew chief to keep control over his aircraft."

"Why is that, sir?"

"A lot of things have changed. Sophistication and galloping technology has changed all that. Nowadays the specialists in the various electronic fields have more status in the Air Force than a crew chief."

"And that's not good?"

The major explained, "Let's just say it's not good when the flight line has to take a back seat."

Thanks to Major Bensen, the flight line had won that battle, but the war raged on. Early the next morning, the major and I walked into Maintenance Control.

Sergeant Conn reported, "Twelve aircraft ready for the first launch, sir."

We proceeded to the line to behold the majestic sight. After walking past the first five aircraft, we saw two puzzled pilots waiting with their gear down the line on two empty spots. The major immediately started to count: "Seven, eight, nine, ten." He counted again to be sure. "Where the hell are the other two birds?"

We found the two *lost sheep* in Hangar Two just as Townley came upon them with the crew chiefs frantically buttoning up access panels.

The major asked, "Sergeant, are you trying to sabotage me?"

"No, sir," Townley answered and started to assist the crew chiefs in installing the panels.

"Then why aren't these birds ready to go?"

"They're ready, except for the panels, sir. Radar worked on them last and they didn't button up."

"Master Sergeant Townley, are you telling me that the flight line isn't responsible for the aircraft?"

Townley remained silent and continued screwing down panels.

The two aircraft missed the launch. Theoretically, it's the crew chief's job to remove and replace all access panels, but in the past radar had cooperated by installing the panels if they worked last on an aircraft.

After a brief session with Colonel Wyler, Major Bensen told me that radar pulled a two-bit stunt on the flight line by not installing panels, but he said, "I couldn't leave Sergeant Townley off the hook though because the flight line has final responsibility for the aircraft. If that ever changes we're in deep trouble."

Other things contributed to the strained relationship between electronics and the flight line—like the selection of the Squadron Airman of the Month. Each month the award went to an airman, picked by a committee of ten NCOs, headed by Master Sergeant Talifano. I learned about the award from Rosy as he admired the three-day pass of an electronics technician, the latest winner. Talking with others, I discovered the electronics area had claimed eight of the last twelve awards, and nobody could recall the last time a crew chief had been chosen.

I queried Townley and he said, "Heck, Lieutenant, I submit a nominee each month, but by the time Talifano and Tench from radar, and Muldoon from armament work him over with all their questions on current political events, he's done."

"Current political events?"

"Yeah, like this month for example, I picked Airman Jones because he had that idea for making those transparent fuel lines so we could find the siphoning problems. You know how that paid off, Lieutenant … well, at the interview, Talifano asked him to name the Secretary of Defense and he couldn't remember, so they voted for that kid from radar."

My conversation with Townley must have rekindled some grave doubts he had about the validity of the award because the next thing I knew, he decided not to submit anymore nominees. Instead, the flight line gave its own award—Crew Chief of the Month. And in addition to a three-day pass, Colonel Wyler agreed to give the winning crew chief a ride in the back seat of one of the B models. Apparently he made this suggestion without first consulting the crew chiefs, because they graciously thanked Sergeant Townley instead of the CO, but as far as I know none ever went for a ride.

When radar heard of Townley's new award for the crew chiefs, they announced a new award—Warrant Officer of the Month.

Townley laughed when I told him, but he refused to openly acknowledge the humor in radar's kidding.

The antics between the flight line and the electronics types didn't go entirely unnoticed by Major Bensen. He announced that he had decided to try a little change: Effective the next day, Sergeant Townley had to send one of his flights with all their gear to Hangar Two, the electronics area. At the same time, Will Shock had to have one of the radar flights move to Hanger One with the crew chiefs.

Will protested, saying, "It won't work out, Major."

The major snorted back, "And why not?"

Sergeant Townley took a firm stand and muttered, "I'm not sending my crew chiefs to live with them squash-heads," but not until the major walked out of hearing range.

The next morning, after the aircraft took off, Sergeant Grobly of A-Flight herded his six crew chiefs and they loaded the toolboxes and other equipment into the back of the blue pickup then headed for Hangar Two. Midway, they passed a blue van filled with radar technicians and their equipment. Airman Bean used sign language to express his sentiments and the radar van driver quickly reciprocated.

At the officers' club that evening, I learned the integration of the flight line and radar was not a spur of the moment decision.

After several drinks, Major Bensen leaned toward me and asked, "What do you think of the change this morning?"

"Oh, I guess something had to be done."

Major Bensen winced. "I didn't do it just to do something, or to prove I'm the boss."

I realized then I had taken his question too lightly.

"As a matter of fact," he continued, "it's something we should have started long before this ... years ago."

Unsure I had heard correctly, I repeated, "Years ago?"

"That's right," he calmly stated. "You see, when the Air Force began cramming all sorts of weapons systems and electronics gear into airplanes, some bright people decided that something was needed in order to manage all that new technology so they wrote Air Force Manual, Sixty-six dash one (AFM 66-1)."

I was familiar with AFM 66-1, the maintenance management bible and in maintenance school we digested every word as gospel.

Major Bensen said, "It separated everything and everybody into nice neat packages. Radar does this and armament does that, and a crew chief does his bit ... pure division of labor. Only problem is the left hand doesn't know what the right hand is doing, or even more importantly ... why? Christ ... how the hell can an airman get any satisfaction these days?"

"Sounds like they thought about everything but the people who have to do the work."

"Exactly! Now, by putting people with different jobs together, it's *just* possible they might talk to each other and understand each other's problems." He paused, and I figured he thought about today's move. He continued, "Well, at any rate, think of our little move today as an experiment."

"It'll be interesting to see how it works out," I said.

We finished our drinks and left the club.

A few days later, a cold, blustery morning, I went to the line and noticed each aircraft carried two external wing tanks. Townley drove by and I hopped into the pickup. The crew chiefs, all in heavy winter jackets with wolf-hair hoods, continued to make the final checks on the aircraft. Townley pulled behind 375 and parked.

I asked, “Something new?”

Townley said, “Yeah, the colonel called control in the middle of the night and ordered the wing tanks hung. Christ … I had to get the day shift out at two in the morning to get them on. I don’t think the major even knows yet.”

“Why the tanks?”

“Make up for lost flying time. We can get an extra half hour on each flight with them on, but, hell, it’s not worth it.”

“How come?”

Townley explained,”We’ll spend more time fooling with tanks than fixing airplanes, Lieutenant. Only the birds scheduled to fly will carry tanks, not the alert birds, so every time we rotate birds to alert, which is every other day, we have to remove the tanks from the birds going on and put them back on the birds coming off alert. And for safety reasons we have to remove the tanks any time we have to jack up a bird or do other maintenance.”

“I can see where it creates a lot of extra work.”

Townley muttered, “That’s not the half of it. The tanks don’t drain out completely so every time we take one off, we’ll have to pull it to the fuel disposal area and empty the excess.”

Townley saw Captain Seimons, the first pilot to come out of Operations so he drove over to him. “Care for a lift, Captain?”

“I sure could use one this morning. I got Two-sixty (260) and I think it’s way down the line.”

“You’re right. Hop on.”

The captain got on the back end of the pickup with his gear and as we reached 260, Townley pointed to the wing tanks then asked, “Your idea to catch up on some flying time, Captain?”

“You must be kidding, Sarge,” Captain Seimons said, before he realized that Townley was putting him on. “You should have heard the other pilots when they found out about the tanks. Can’t say I blame them either. Flying with tanks is like driving a bus.”

We laughed at the captain’s analogy.

Captain Seimons asked, “Does Major Bensen know yet?”

“Don’t know,” Townley replied.

“Well, it should be interesting … very interesting indeed.”

I guess Captain Seimons knew Major Bensen pretty well.

When we saw the colonel and Major Harmon come out the back door of the Operations building, heading toward the waiting aircraft, Townley said, "They're running late," then headed over to pick them up.

As he drove, I saw Major Bensen emerge from the hangar and begin to head to the aircraft.

Major Bensen arrived first and as we pulled up, we heard him say, "You didn't consult me about flying tanks."

The colonel looked surprised and didn't reply at first. "Since when does the chief of maintenance determine how we fly? Besides, Major Harmon here agrees that it's a good way to recoup flying time, all because it took you so long to get them leaks figured out."

"So Major Harmon thinks it's a good idea too, huh? Wait till the pilots hear about this."

Major Harmon said, "Now, Harry, it's not necessary to go that far. It's an operational decision. We're committed to a lot more hours than we've flown so far this quarter."

Major Bensen said, "And I'm committed to a lot more maintenance than we'll have time for if we have to screw around with tanks."

Colonel Wyler got louder. "The airplane was designed to carry tanks, Major. Are you forgetting?"

"That's an old aircraft, Colonel … maybe five years ago … sure, but not now … on every flight, every day. That's too much. I think we should talk about it."

The colonel commanded, "Fly the tanks, Major."

"Do you think Major Harmon would have made it back that day he hit the gulls if he had tanks?"

This irritated the colonel and he shouted, "Fly the tanks, Major!"

We could see the crew chief getting nervous so Townley drifted over to the next aircraft.

The next day, Sergeant Townley grabbed every spare moment to instruct the newer crew chiefs about hanging tanks. The day was uneventful until the last aircraft of the afternoon flight appeared.

"Here she comes, hotter than a firecracker," the crew chief announced, referring to the F-106 approach as being *hot* because it didn't have flaps to slow it down like most other jets.

I asked, "Who's the pilot?"

"Lieutenant Parks," Sergeant Townley replied.

A few moments later, Parks made a picture perfect landing, two white puffs of smoke rising where the tires met the concrete. The aircraft barreled down the runway and the chute door opened. The little pilot chute popped out, but the main chute failed to emerge.

The crew chief, in a frightened tone, said, "Lieutenant Parks got himself a big problem."

We watched as the little pilot chute managed to pull the main chute part way out of the compartment, but there it flopped from side to side still not deployed as the aircraft quickly approached the end of the runway, brakes squealing, but not slowing down.

The crew chief announced, "He better jettison those tanks."

I struggled to recall the procedure I learned in flight school. *Should he drop the tail hook and try to grab the restraining cable?* If the hook missed or bounced over the cable, he would have to take the restraining barrier, a risky proposition at best in the F-106. If the rubber barrier held, the gear would still be severely damaged. If it didn't hold, the aircraft would end up off the runway in the boondocks. I remembered safe procedure called for jettisoning external tanks because of the potential fire hazard.

As the hook fell to grab the cable, a shower of sparks rose from the runway. Parks had either forgotten about the tanks or wrongly decided to keep them on.

I heard a loud squeal, and then the crew chief shouted, "He got the cable!"

Within minutes a crowd gathered at the aircraft. The crew chief placed a set of protective screens around both hissing wheels.

Townley warned everyone, "It'll take a few minutes for the heat to build up, so stay clear of the gear.

A flight line vehicle towed a platform into place and everyone climbed up to inspect the chute. Colonel Wyler and Major Bensen examined the partially deployed main chute which slid back into the compartment.

"Looks like it tried to open," the CO said.

Sergeant Paris, from the drag chute shop and a young black airman began checking to see if the chute was properly packed.

Captain Lickle, the flight safety officer ordered, "Don't touch that chute till we have a chance to examine it in the shop."

From the rear, Sergeant Townley spoke up. "Nothing's wrong with the chute." He came forward. "Here's the problem," plucking an almost invisible piece of nylon thread from a little protruding screw inside the compartment. "The chute opened all right, but it got caught on this screw."

Colonel Wyler exclaimed, "Well, I'll be!"

Just then, the left wheel exploded, frightening everyone on the platform but Townley.

That evening Sergeant Pardini and I burned the midnight oil in records preparing an emergency report to be sent out first thing in the morning. Captain Lickle had already wired a brief directive to all operating squadrons, trying to explain how and why a little screw had almost caused a major accident.

As we struggled with the report, Major Bensen came in and announced, "We found two more birds with loose screws … Two-fifty-one (251) and Two-sixty (260). Include that in the report." As I started to revise the report, he added, "That's the kind of thing that gives maintenance officers gray hair."

I nodded in agreement, studying the major's mop of gray hair and said, "You would think the designers could anticipate that sort of thing."

The major laughed then said to Pardini, "Tell him, Sarge."

Sergeant Pardini smiled. "I remember one aircraft where they put the gear handle right next to the drag chute handle, until one pilot put the gear up instead of releasing the chute." Sergeant Pardini, who had a large family, then made a profound statement. "It's too bad the guy who invented hinges for refrigerators isn't an aircraft designer."

The major said, "Yeah, we'll probably see more little things happen, like today." His words sounded ominous and my expression must have begged for an explanation because he said, "Think of the F-106 as an aging actress. The structural modifications are like a good face lift, but you can't stop the aging process. Sooner or later it takes its toll."

After Sergeant Pardini left, the major said, "Listen, Joe, there's something else I'm concerned about. Remember that black airman from the drag chute shop out there with Sergeant Paris today?"

"Yes, sir."

"That's Airman Jones … Percy Jones. I've never seen him so down before. I could be wrong … maybe it was the incident, but something else might be bothering him too. Would you do me a favor tomorrow, and see what you can find out?"

"Sure."

Major Bensen gave me a lead. "I don't know if it has any bearing, but Percy just got married a month ago."

The next morning, as soon as the aircraft were off, I casually strolled into the drag chute shop and found Airman Jones alone, sewing an insignia on a pilot's flight suit. He told me that Sergeant Paris went out to hang some chutes to dry.

Hoping to get a rise out of Jones, who seemed a bit depressed, I said, "I always wondered who did the sewing for the bachelors."

He nodded and continued sewing.

I prodded more. "I see you're not a bachelor."

"No, sir … just got married, but I think I made a mistake."

"I'm sure it's a big change."

"Yeah, you run into a lot of things you don't expect. I figured we'd be able to find a place to live on the Cape, near the base, but no luck. I don't have enough time in the Air Force to rate base housing."

"Where are you living?"

"With my wife's mother in Fall River."

"That's pretty far."

"It's not that it's far. I think we'd be better off on our own … away from families."

"No luck finding anything on the Cape, huh?"

He grinned for the first time. "Lieutenant, if you was black, you wouldn't need to ask that question."

I reported what I learned to Major Bensen and he looked disgusted, but not surprised. "What do you think?"

"Base housing?"

"No, I don't like that," he said. "We'd have to pull some strings and it might be worse for Jones."

The major went house hunting in several of the nearby towns and found plenty of vacancies, until he revealed his young, just-married airman was black.

He said, "If the United States Air Force isn't good enough … maybe there's another way."

We donned our dress blue uniforms and went to visit one of the major's friends, also the president of a local Chamber of Commerce who said, "If I knew you wanted this, I wouldn't have showed up. There are no negro families living here."

But the major wouldn't be denied and with a little persuasion and some reluctant assistance, we finally found a cozy, three room house that wouldn't wreck a young airman's budget.

Major Bensen always did things like that to help the airmen and NCOs in the squadron. Realizing that people are often hesitant to reveal their personal burdens, he stayed alert for signs of something festering—like the time he noticed an airman from the engine shop half-asleep while working on an engine. After a casual discussion, the airman revealed that for the past week, he had been trying to get someone out to fix an inoperative furnace in his base house. The major called base housing and the furnace got fixed before the airman went home that day.

So it came as no great mystery when I overheard several airmen refer to Major Bensen as the *airmen's godfather*.

Chapter 6

The Russians Are Coming

A week didn't go by that someone would remind us about the Russians sitting off the coast, monitoring our every move, usually the same solitary Russian trawler anchored outside our territorial waters. When two more trawlers moved into place, we knew something would happen, and shortly afterward, the Russians started coming in with their long range bombers—subsonic Bisons and Bears. Each time we scrambled the alert aircraft to meet the threat, sometimes only a lone bomber then other times a whole formation of the block long meat grinders. Once met, the Russians would wave to our pilots, turn and return to their bases. Major Bensen said the Russians always tested us like that to assess our reaction time and capabilities.

After one encounter, Major Harmon commented the Russians had used some kind of new electronic countermeasure gear which made detecting them very difficult. On another scramble, one of our pilots reported sighting several old vintage bombers converted into tankers. The squadron considered this information very significant because, of 950 Bisons and Bears, we knew that only around 200 had enough range to reach the United States and return. These tankers gave the Russians the capability to bring in a lot more of their bomber forces.

With the Russians coming in more than ever before, a sense of urgency permeated the squadron. The pilots, who normally dreaded ting out the boredom at the alert barn, now volunteered for the A betting pool started—the winner to be the first pilot to sight est Russian bomber, the Backfire. We expected the Russians r new supersonic airplane, and if the reports proved true, ne capabilities. It could come in very high or right on this new, ground-hugging, radar-ducking attacker ble foe.

The pace in maintenance quickened and we repaired the aircraft with renewed conviction. To keep us ready for any contingency, Colonel Wyler called several *Sunday Punches*, and I even witnessed the usually stoic Captain Roberts sporting a big smile.

Not everyone took the Russian threat seriously, Rosy being one exception. One day, Sergeant Taft and I waited in supply for Major Bensen. He had asked us to compile a list of critical items, those parts in short supply which usually took several days to obtain.

Rosy, who helped gather the information, stated out of the blue, "Everybody knows that if anything ever happens, it'll be over quick, not with bombers, but with nuclear missiles."

I commented, "We can detect missiles the instant they're fired and then get our aircraft up."

"What about submarine missiles?"

I wasn't sure about the Russian submarine potential or even if we knew the location of their subs. "Even if it does start with missiles, they'll still need manned aircraft to evaluate the damage, and that's where we come in. We intercept the bombers."

"Well, assuming we do get some birds off the ground," Rosy continued, "how can they stay up till the Russians get here?"

"Refuel with tankers."

He shot back, "What tankers? All our tankers will be escorting our own bomber force."

Sergeant Taft, who took a mild interest in our discussion, came to my rescue. "Maybe the Russians will pull a sneaky Pete and come with bombers instead of missiles."

"Hey, I got it," Rosy stated. "What if some other country fires a missile and we think it's the Russians?"

Sergeant Taft responded with, "Hey, I got it, what if Major Bensen comes in and you're not finished with that list?"

Rosy put his nose back in his work and finished just as the major walked through the door.

About halfway through with the review of critical items the base sirens sounded, one long blast of about ten seconds followed by three short ones.

After the pattern repeated, the major said, "That's the base sabotage alert."

Rosy suggested, "Maybe it's just a drill."

The major said, "No, it can't be. I would have been notified if somebody was playing games. Come on, Joe, let's go see what Control knows."

Once we arrived in Control and saw Sergeant Conn on the phone, Major Bensen asked, "What's it all about?"

"Don't know yet, sir," Conn said shrugging his shoulders. "I'm on the phone now with Ops and they want all the birds off the ground. Colonel Wyler wants you to come right over."

We paused between the hangar and operations to watch an air police vehicle racing down the road toward the squadron. The base sirens screamed, and at each quarter mile along the road, a vehicle stopped and two armed APs jumped out.

We met the colonel at the side door.

The major asked, "What's happening?"

Colonel Wyler exclaimed, "I don't know yet, but it's something big! It could be the Russians. How many birds can we get off right now, Harry?"

"All but three. We're moving them out to the spots now."

"Good."

Several pilots whisked by with their gear and Janice appeared at the far end of the hall. "Colonel," she called, "General Braddock is on the phone."

We followed as the colonel scurried back to the office. He picked up the receiver from the desk. "Yes, General … yes, sir. I see uh-huh …uh-huh, yes." The colonel's face turned a shade of violet as he stood listening. A pained look spread over his face and he fixed his eyes on Major Bensen. Then he slumped into his swivel chair and slowly turned toward the window.

Tractors began pulling the aircraft to the spots where the pilots waited. "Yes, sir … yes, General."

Facing the apron and looking out his big window the colonel said, "Someone discovered jet fuel in the storm drain system. The whole base is sitting on a bomb and they traced the fuel to us … to Hangar Two." Then slowly the colonel turned around. The look of defeat turned to rage and he yelled, "You better have a good explanation, Major!"

We left without a word, and I realize now that Major Bensen probably had it all figured out before we left the building. We had been flying for several weeks using the external wing tanks and as Sergeant Townley warned, they posed problems.

Each time the flight line removed a tank, gallons of unused fuel still remained and had to be emptied into the fuel disposal tank buried on the side of Hangar One. This presented a special problem for A-Flight, relegated by Major Bensen to Hangar Two, because each time one of their crew chiefs removed a tank from his bird in Hangar Two, he faced the ordeal of pulling it on a little yellow dolly all the way across the windy apron to the far side of Hangar One. Their salvation finally came when one weary, but investigative, crew chief discovered a convenient storm drain right alongside of Hangar Two. The jet fuel, being lighter than water, floated on top and found its way around the entire base.

Warrant Officer Shock was quick to remind the major: "Don't say I didn't warn you. I knew it wouldn't work out having those crew chiefs in our hangar. It's been one incident after another ever since they came. I've been expecting something like this to happen."

"I think the colonel agrees with you, Will," the major said.

Will continued talking with obvious satisfaction, "Well, it *just* hasn't worked out, Major. I guess they don't have too much in common. Are you going to retract the move then?"

"No."

With disbelief in his voice, Will asked, "No … why not?"

"Let's give it a little more time, Will. People have a tendency to resist change, even when it's best."

Not only did Major Bensen refuse to move A-Flight back to Hangar One and the radar flight back to Hangar Two, but I didn't hear about any reprimands or punishment. Then later that afternoon Major Bensen passed (quite by coincidence I think) the nervous young crew chief who came up with the idea to dispose of the fuel. The major nodded his head and gave the young lad a most approving wink. I swear that crew chief smiled constantly for two weeks and time would prove he became one of the best crew chiefs in the squadron.

A few nights later at the officers' club, Major Bensen brought up the episode. "I guess you're wondering why I didn't raise a lot of hell with that airman, or Sergeant Townley."

If anything, I was beginning to learn Major Bensen usually had a good reason for decisions. "I think I understand." His smile of satisfaction urged me to continue. "As bad a blunder as it was, the airman did show initiative and ingenuity, and you didn't want to do anything that would discourage anyone from trying in the future."

"Not only him, but anybody," the major quickly added. "It was a blunder … a total fiasco is more exact, but it tells me that the airman was thinking and that he had some say in deciding how to do his job. It's very important to maintain that sense of individual freedom and initiative, Joe. That's the basis for important ideas and contributions. If you force people to work in an environment where they're afraid to do anything unless somebody orders them, you end up with only a bunch of warm bodies."

I nodded that I understood.

He continued, "That's the reason we keep maintenance control on a coordinating level, rather than a point of decision making and control. I don't want a bunch of master sergeants giving orders from inside an office."

"I think the Air Force has other plans," I said.

A frown came across the major's face. "I heard the nasty rumor … computers, huh?"

"That's the grand plan and what everyone said in maintenance school."

Major Bensen shook his head. "Well, I probably won't be here to see it, but you will."

The next day, I walked into records after lunch and noticed one of the clerk typists energetically spit shining a pair of scruffy looking shoes so I asked, "Heavy date?"

"No, sir," he replied, looking to Sergeant Pardini for some sort of reassurance.

Pardini said, "I told him it was okay, Lieutenant. It's for the inspection Saturday."

"Inspection … what inspection?"

"Didn't you get the word, Lieutenant? Sergeant Talifano called. The colonel ordered an inspection in first class blues for Saturday at oh-nine-hundred."

Next door in supply, Rosy appeared as if in a state of shock, and when he finally saw me, he asked, "What do you think, Lieutenant? Can you believe it, huh? Ever hear of a formal inspection in ADC? Sergeant Taft says the CO must think he's still in SAC."

Sergeant Taft, who stood nearby reading a bulky supply manual, peered over the top and gave Rosy a look that warned him to speak for himself.

"Isn't it a little short notice? It's already Wednesday afternoon."

Rosy quickly agreed. "Yeah, it sure is. I think the CO's trying to *SACimcize* the squadron."

The bizarre remark caused Sergeant Taft to go into a juggling act with the big supply manual. Finally, Taft's lack of dexterity showed, and the manual crashed to the floor.

That evening Janice and I went to see a good western playing at the base movie theater. I missed most of the action because she kept telling me about Sergeant Talifano's extravagant preparations for the big inspection. She said the first sergeant seemed really enthused and after researching a number of Air Force manuals, had asked Janice to type a letter of instructions, outlining the correct protocol for the dress inspection. The letter, which would go out to all the NCOs first thing in the morning, had a colorful sketch attached showing each section where to line up in front of Hangar One. Janice couldn't remember if the maintenance officers lined up on the left or the right, only that he put us up front. She said that Talifano told her he put the electronics section up front too, hoping to make a good first impression on the CO.

On Thursday and Friday, I witnessed two of the busiest days ever in the squadron. Not that a lot of maintenance work took place, on the contrary, very little of that happened, but a lot of activity occurred. People rushed out to get uniforms cleaned and pressed, crew chiefs scurried to the barbershop between sorties and a lot of last minute shopping for missing uniform items. Some of the old-timers claimed they had never stood an inspection in ADC, and many of them had to purchase items of clothing which had been lost, misplaced or didn't fit anymore. I talked to one grumbling NCO who had to buy a whole new uniform, except for the shoes.

By Friday afternoon the base PX sold out of blue ties and dress shirts. Rosy reported that several ambitious crew chiefs had been scalping those items in the flight line lounge.

After the major learned that pilots were not to stand inspection, he became quite concerned. Janice told me he besieged the colonel all day Friday, reminding him about his *one big team* concept and arguing if that was the case, the whole team should stand inspection, not just maintenance. Janice said the colonel ignored him and seemed to enjoy the major's frustration.

On Saturday morning at eight forty-five, the maintenance troops fell in according to plan in front of Hangar One. Everyone looked cold and a few couldn't stop shivering as each NCO completed his roll call and reported to Major Bensen.

Then in a voice from bygone days the major called out, "Squaa … dron … at ease!"

We shivered more and waited. At nine sharp the rear door from Operations opened and the colonel and Talifano emerged.

Major Bensen, reluctance still in his voice, yelled, "Squadron-Ahh-tenshun!"

The major made his best effort with the salute then followed close behind Talifano as the colonel commenced the inspection. The colonel hurried by the officers with hardly a second glance, but the enlisted men received closer scrutiny. I watched from the corner of my eye as he straightened ties, brushed off dandruff, noted poorly shined shoes, and pointed to the blood on several hastily shaved airmen. Sergeant Talifano wrote it all down on his clipboard.

The CO passed behind me several times, and I waited for him to come to the first row of flight line airmen. Earlier, in front of the hangar and before we got in formation, I noticed the uniforms of the crew chiefs. They looked truly immaculate with their brilliant spit-shined shoes, black as the ace of spades and each one mirror perfect. It seemed almost unbelievable.

At last the colonel finished the mechanical shops then turned to start down the first row of the flight line. I turned my head, daring more than I should. The colonel's expression said it all—probably the most eye-catching display of military perfection he had ever seen. Even Sergeant Talifano looked flabbergasted.

Right after the inspection, Rosy, who had labored countless hours for just a mediocre shine, managed to coax the secret from one of the crew chiefs.

"Unbelievable," I heard him say. "A monumental deception … it's just an ordinary brush shine and a last second touch-up with a five-day deodorant pad."

On a windy March day during the next week an incident happened that exposed one aspect of the insidious nature of corrosion. Seven aircraft had already boomed off. Only 251, our oldest interceptor, and 280, recently returned from the depot, remained, waiting for the call from operations.

Townley slowly moved the pickup to one side behind the two birds. Aircraft 251 got the call first and taxied out. Anticipating the call for 280 next, the crew chief pushed the button to start the mobile air compressor. The unit started, and then roared like an angry bear, building up excess pressure until the relief horn sounded and the unit stalled out.

Sergeant Townley jumped out to help the crew chief as I watched from the truck. The sergeant gave the compressor another try, only to have the same thing happen. After a brief discussion, Townley and the crew chief started for the compressor on the next spot. But Lieutenant Holt yelled from the cockpit, waving them back to the aircraft.

I guessed that a call came from Operations and Holt wanted to go. Without the mobile compressor for a start, Holt would have to use the aircraft's compressed air bottle. Townley went to the aircraft and I watched as the sergeant told Holt what he already knew. If the aircraft's compressed air got depleted during the start, there would be none left in flight, for at least one thing I could think of—blowing down the gear if it got stuck in the up position. Lieutenant Holt nodded and Townley walked away, accepting the fact there wasn't much he could do if a pilot wanted to violate a safety-of-flight rule.

The engine started and the instant the crew chief pulled the chocks, Holt applied power and the bird jumped out. He turned sharply for the runway, but then I heard a resounding CRACK. I looked and the lower wheel assembly of the right main gear had broken off and started cart-wheeling toward Townley and the crew chief. I sat petrified and watched as Townley ducked behind the yellow compressor. The crew chief fell to the concrete and the wheel went tumbling past. The aircraft, right wing tilted low, continued on with the stump of the strut digging through the concrete. The sheared wheel bounced and hopped across the open apron, finally losing momentum a few feet from Hangar One. Meanwhile, Holt had managed to stop the aircraft and climbed out of the cockpit. Then he slid down the high side of the fuselage.

I stayed on line while Townley supervised the jacking operation then we headed for Hangar One. A crowd had gathered around the table where the severed wheel assembly rested. Sergeant Townley pushed his way through the on-looking airmen. Colonel Wyler, Major Bensen, and Captain Lickle stood around the table, examining the strut and wheel assembly.

Colonel Wyler said, "What a nasty break," as he ran his hand across the ragged edges of the metal.

Major Bensen handed Townley a magnifying glass, "Take a look, Sarge."

Townley examined the fracture closely then announced, "It's a fatigue failure, caused by repeated overload."

Captain Lickle asked, "How do you know it's caused by overload?"

"Each one of these raised lips indicates an overload," Townley said, pointing to the metal in a darker, discolored area of the break. "The problem started here," he said, pointing to a tiny pit mark on the surface of the strut. "Then it moved in until the strut was weakened and finally cracked right here," running his finger across a line which separated the discolored area from a clean, shiny section of the break.

Again, Captain Lickle asked a question, "Are you saying that the crack has been there for some time?"

I saw the colonel give Major Bensen an accusing look.

"Maybe," Townley answered. "It's hard to say about corrosion."

The colonel seemed surprised. "Corrosion?"

"Yes, sir. It can take a long time to develop or it can happen just like that," Townley said, snapping his fingers. "You can't detect it with the naked eye or even a magnifying glass. If you saw this strut before it cracked, the spot where the fatigue started would look like any other tiny pit marks on the strut."

The colonel asked, "Well, how can we check them?"

"We can use a penetrating dye here in the squadron, but it's not perfect. They're supposed to check them electronically at the depot.

The colonel said, "This bird just came back from the depot a few weeks ago."

"We know," Major Bensen said. "We're lucky it didn't happen on takeoff or landing."

"Landing? How many birds do we have still up, Major?"

"Eight ... all with two tanks each."

The colonel looked excited. "Captain Lickle, get on the horn to every pilot! I want all excess fuel burned off before they come in! I want to see the softest landings they've ever made!"

"Yes, sir!"

"No sharp turns after they land!"

As he headed for Ops, Captain Lickle hollered out, "Yes, sir!"

The colonel yelled back to him. "One more thing! Notify crash and rescue too!"

The aircraft came in like landing on eggs and as soon as the last bird touched down safely, Townley remarked, "They should have dropped the tanks in the dump."

I said, "At least we won't be seeing them anymore."

That evening Major Bensen and I grabbed a quick dinner at the club and returned to the squadron to watch the flight line check for cracks. The test, a tedious and time consuming procedure, marked off each strut with squares like in a checkerboard then each square inch carefully cleaned and a fluorescent penetrating dye applied. The dye penetrated into any miniscule cracks, undetectable by the naked eye. Then after a set time, the area got wiped clean and carefully examined with an ultra violet light, looking for dye seeping back out of any telltale crack.

Sergeant Townley said, "The test could still miss a crack if it happened to be under the surface of the strut."

The dangerous nature of corrosion became apparent to me.

After the first three birds checked out okay, Major Bensen appeared a little more relaxed. He seemed more relieved when a red-faced master sergeant by the name of Biggs tracked us down in Hangar Three to report that the struts on 260, one of the older birds, were in good shape.

After Sergeant Biggs left, I said, "First time I ever saw him. I didn't realize we had a master sergeant on the night shift."

"Yeah, Sergeant Biggs is a special case," the major said. "He's an alcoholic."

"I thought I smelled something."

"He has a few when he's off duty, but he's learned to control it, and he's responsible."

"No problems then?"

The major explained, "It seems to be working out pretty good on the night shift. Besides, by working at night it gives him time to get over to the hospital three afternoons a week. They have a little clinic over there and he seems to be making good progress. I hope he gets it completely licked before he retires next year."

The inspections seemed to be going well so we went into the flight line lounge for coffee. Sergeant Townley called from the alert barn and the major took the call in the vacant flight line officer's cubicle.

"Okay. Keep me posted," I heard him say. When I saw him come out I knew our expectations were premature. "The second bird they checked at the barn had three cracks in the right strut."

"There are two spare struts at base supply … a right and a left. We used the other right for Two-eighty (280)."

"I'll have Biggs get somebody to go pick them up. We might as well bring both over. We'll probably need the other one before we're finished."

But by two in the morning no more cracks were found and only one bird remained to be checked.

Sergeant Townley returned from the barn and said, "There's something I want to get off my chest before I leave tonight."

"Aircraft Two-eighty (280)?"

The major guessed right, surprising the husky sergeant.

"Yeah, right. You know I never did have too much faith in depots … now this incident today with the strut. Christ … they had that bird out there for nearly two weeks and the report came back giving it a clean bill of health."

"And?"

"Well, hell, I know that can't be right."

The major asked "What do you recommend?"

"Give me a bird for two weeks. Any bird and I'll—"

"Two weeks? I'm not a miracle man, Sarge, but I'll see what I can do."

I suggested, "After what happened today, the colonel might understand."

"I hope so," Major Bensen said then paused. "If he doesn't, you'll get an aircraft anyway."

"Good," Townley said.

The next morning we learned that the last bird had one cracked strut, a left one, and as luck would have it, the one we had. The strut got replaced, and the bird made ready for the morning launch.

After the strut incident and the discovery of corrosion, I think Major Bensen really had high hopes of convincing Colonel Wyler of the need to let maintenance take a close look at one of the birds, perhaps not for an entire two weeks as Sergeant Townley requested, but for some uninterrupted period of time. At any rate, I think that's why he invited me to sit in on the meeting with the CO.

On the way to the colonel's office, I almost wore out my welcome, forcing the major to wait several times, as I stopped to buff shine my flight boots on the back of my calves. When Janice saw me enter with Major Bensen, she smiled and looked impressed.

As we entered the office, she gave a tug on my sleeve and whispered, "I told you he liked you."

Well prepared, Major Bensen used 280 as a prime example and expressed Sergeant Townley's sentiments about the quality of preventive maintenance performed at the depot. The colonel sat mute, but attentive as the major talked about corrosion and the need to examine critical parts in all the inaccessible places on the aircraft. I sat with the grimmest look I could muster.

Finally, the major got to the point. "Maintenance needs to have an aircraft for two weeks, sir."

"Two weeks! My God, do you realize what you're asking? That's impossible."

"Okay, then," Major Bensen said, "we'll do what we can in one week."

The colonel gave him a school teacher look. "Major, I'm sure you realize we're just beginning the second quarter. The first quarter was a real disaster."

"We had the leaks sir. Once we cleared that up, the flying went fine."

The colonel held up a pile of papers in each hand. "I know, but look at all these memos from ADC. We have one of the lowest in commission rates in ADC."

Major Bensen replied, "We also have one of the most corrosive atmospheres. The Cape sticks out into the ocean like a—"

"Don't give me a geography lesson, Major. Our location is precisely the point. We protect the most critical sector in ADC … New York City, Philadelphia, Boston, the industrial heart of our nation! Why do you think the Russians are out there, probing and testing? That's all the more reason why we can't have birds sitting out of commission while you go on a witch hunt."

Major Bensen exploded. "Witch hunt? Is that what you think this is all about?"

I followed him out of the office and Janice looked disappointed that my first encounter with the colonel had ended in failure.

Ironically, the Russian maneuvers ceased almost as suddenly as they began, and nobody ever did win the pool for sighting the Backfire bomber.

Rosy seemed sure that it came and said, "It's too fast for the old *Six* to even smell, Lieutenant."

Chapter 7

The Colonel's Bird

April came, bringing everything new and fresh to the Cape. To Sergeant Pardini, spring meant cleaning out files and updating the technical orders. We had just completed that chore when Captain Johnson, the squadron historian and information officer, called.

"Joe, this is Bill Johnson. Listen, I need some information on aircraft Three-eighty-one (381). Can you help me?"

"Sure. What is it?"

"Today I flew Three-eighty-one (381) and noticed that the flight hours on the bird approached nearly seven thousand ... six thousand, nine hundred and fifty to be exact. Cripes! That might be some kind of a record!"

"That's a lot of hours."

"Yeah, I wondered if you had a way to find out how that stacks up against any other Darts."

"In the squadron?"

"No, I know that's more than any other bird in the squadron. I mean in ADC."

"Well, that's a big order, but I'll do my best."

The captain exclaimed, "Great! Listen, can you expedite it?"

"Sure."

The task sounded difficult, but Sergeant Pardini had the telephone number of every records section in ADC and after checking, I found out that 381 did in fact accumulate more flying time than any other F-106. Only one other aircraft in a squadron in South Carolina came close, within thirty hours of 381. I gave Captain Johnson the good news.

"Hey, that's terrific. Thanks a million, Joe."

Janice said it took Colonel Wyler a few days to get used to Captain Johnson's proposal of publicizing the fact that 381 neared the 7000 hour mark. Johnson talked about all the recognition the squadron would get, but the colonel remained cool to the idea. The captain added a new twist, a crowning ceremony upon completing

7000 flight hours and with the squadron commander flying the aircraft. She said the colonel finally decided that a little recognition would be good to boost morale.

Old 381 soon became known as the CO's bird and true to form the colonel flew her at every opportunity. And when he got bogged down with administrative duties, one of the other pilots took her up to keep the hours moving right along.

Sergeant Conn in Control painted his little metal 381 a bright red and even added an eagle decal to each wing.

Noticing the extra attention given 381, Major Bensen spoke to Conn, "There are no special airplanes in this squadron. "Treat that bird like all the rest."

Airman Panza, the crew chief of 381, took real pride that his bird would be honored by Air Force wide recognition. Sergeant Townley mentioned that the young airman only had one gripe each time the colonel flew the bird.

I asked,"What's that?"

"Well, Lieutenant, the colonel has this thing about windshields."

Everyone seemed to be cooperating in the effort to log hours on 381. Whenever Sergeant Conn offered the aircraft to Operations for alert duty, where it may sit for days without accumulating any time, Major Harmon turned it down. Even Sergeant Talifano got into the act because the colonel told him to work closely with Captain Johnson on the arrangements for the big ceremony.

Sergeant Townley didn't seem at all infatuated with 381 so one time I asked him about the aircraft.

Without explaining he said, "Heck, Three-eighty-one (381) is special, that's for sure, Lieutenant, but she's no prize. She's a lemon."

After that, I decided to do a little research of my own. I reviewed the records of 381 for three years back. First I found that it had more safety-of-flight write ups by far, than any of the other aircraft. After correcting such a malfunction, an aircraft usually requires several test flights, each longer than a normal sortie before being released to operations. That accounted for one reason 381 had so much time. Then, by accident, I discovered that 381 rarely stood alert duty.

Sergeant Conn confirmed my suspicion when he said, "That's right, Lieutenant. Operations won't take an aircraft for alert once it gets a reputation for safety-of-flight write ups."

The conclusion seemed obvious. The squadron prepared to honor not the best, but possibly the worst aircraft in ADC, if not the entire Air Force.

After one particular flight, Airman Panza came into supply to order a main oil pump, saying, "The colonel wrote the bird up for oil pressure fluctuates below safe operating limits in flight."

By then Sergeant Taft had gotten so excited about old 381, it came as no surprise when he ordered the pump on the highest priority. But early the next morning, a call from base supply disappointed him, informing us delivery of the pump would be at least three days.

I walked into maintenance control as Major Bensen began giving instructions to Sergeant Conn to give the bird to armament for practice loading of nuclear weapons.

The major checked the clock on the wall and said, "One more thing, have Sergeant Townley tow the bird to Hangar Four in the next ten minutes."

"Yes, sir."

The major added, "Very slowly, too."

Conn echoed, "Yes, sir, very slowly."

Satisfied and sounding like some sort of trap had been set, the major said, "Now, let's go have some breakfast, Joe."

That evening Janice told me how the colonel took the bait. She said she heard him mumbling to himself as he stood at the window while they towed 381 along the apron to the armament hangar. Then, he told her to get Major Bensen.

She happened to know we had just entered the mess and told the colonel. That's when the trap got sprung because she told me the colonel hopped down the stairs. The pilots had just emptied out of the mess when the colonel came rushing in.

Major Bensen smiled. "Well, good morning, Colonel, and a good morning it is. Ten birds on the line ready to go."

"Yes, that's good, but what about Three-eighty-one (381)?"

"Three-eighty-one (381) … let me think. Oh yes, I remember. She needs an oil pump or something like that." Then, looking to me for confirmation, the major said, "Should come in soon."

I confirmed, "Yes, sir … three days … it's a critical item."

Politely, the colonel said, "Listen, Harry, we can't let Three-eighty-one (381) sit for three days."

It was the first time I heard him call the major by his first name.

Then, looking at the two eggs the cook placed in front of him and ignoring the colonel's urgency, the major said, "Maybe the pump will come in sooner."

The colonel snapped, "And maybe not, so I've decided to take a pump from another aircraft."

The major admonished the CO. "Colonel, I can't believe you said that. Remember our understanding? You agreed … your solemn word that I have the final say about cannibalization."

"I know, Major, but this is a special situation."

Major Bensen alluded to a covenant the colonel committed to which gave the chief of maintenance, unquestioned control over cannibalization. For some very good reasons, cannibalization is the dirtiest word in the maintenance vernacular, because if unchecked or uncontrolled, it can cause havoc in a squadron. Robbing one aircraft to get another in commission can result in duplication of work, requiring twice as much time to do repairs and compounding the chance of maintenance error. From an operational standpoint, cannibalization can also backfire, because swapping parts can adversely affect the performance of an otherwise good aircraft.

The major reminded the colonel of all these things with such conviction that he almost unwittingly succeeded.

"I still don't think you're getting the big picture, Major," said the colonel, "so I want Three-eighty-one (381) in commission today."

"Well, okay," the major said.

I know he faked a disappointed look, but he only did it until the colonel left the mess.

Sergeant Townley got his wish and selected aircraft 260 to be cannibalized for the oil pump. Aircraft 260 had been giving the flight line fits with flight control sluggish write ups and Townley reasoned that if he had the bird for a few days they might be able to find the cause of the problems.

On its next flight, 381 had another problem and needed a hydraulic pump. Sergeant Conn reluctantly approached the major with the recommendation that the hydraulic pump also be removed from 260.

The major agreed, "Why certainly."

I saw the surprise on Conn's face.

Even before the oil pump came in, 381 had other problems and needed more parts. And each time, the major so graciously approved the cannibalization of 260 that Sergeant Conn remarked, "It's just not like the major to let a bird get raped like that."

Airman Panza spent so much time bragging that Major Bensen had set 260 aside to provide parts for his bird, that several envious crew chiefs decided to see for themselves. They walked away from 260 unchallenged with a few minor parts. The word spread quickly and the parts got bigger and bigger: Somebody jacked-up the aircraft and took both main gear. Airman Higgins, had a nose wheel shimmy problem with aircraft 400, so he took the nose gear. It didn't take Panza long to realize that 260 had a nice, unscratched windshield and he took the entire canopy and put it on 381.

The colonel congratulated Panza. "Good work, son. You're setting a fine example for the other crew chiefs."

For some unknown reason, Sergeant Singly removed the engine. And even the aircraft panels began to disappear. Warrant Officer Shock became more and more concerned as each day the decimation of 260 took place before his very eyes in Hangar Two. Finally, as a precaution, he instructed his NCOs to remove the electronic boxes before they too disappeared.

Aircraft 260 soon became a true *Hangar Queen*, a mere skeleton of her old self, and on one of our frequent parts inventories, Sergeant Taft said, "That aircraft will never fly again, Lieutenant."

If it went any further, I'm sure 260 would have disappeared completely, presenting me as supply officer with the unprecedented task of removing an operational aircraft from the Air Force inventory. Fortunately for me, Major Bensen restricted any further cannibalization.

The decision to stop robbing 260 and get it back in commission meant of course that old 381 no longer had a donor. The first time she needed a part to keep the hours moving, the colonel called Major Bensen, only this time the major fully asserted himself as the chief of maintenance and refused to cannibalize 260 any further.

Realizing his fortitude, the CO declared, "Then you better get Two-sixty (260) back in commission and quick. We can't have two birds sitting around."

Getting all the parts for 260 became a real challenge. When we first began, Sergeant Taft and I had compiled a list of parts three pages long, but when all the parts came in, we discovered we needed more and after that, even more. The list never seemed to be finished. Then we had a problem with missing panels which had to be custom made and fitted by Sergeant Jones in the sheet metal shop.

During this period the latent talent of Airman Buckley, alias *Scarecrow One*, surfaced. Each time 381 needed a part to keep her going, or we discovered that 260 still needed what we hopefully thought would be the *last* part, Buckley would come to supply and offer to search the bins over at base.

The first time we needed a fuel control assembly, Sergeant Taft said, "I already checked base supply. You'd be just wasting time."

Buckley replied, "Can't hurt to try, Sarge."

"Well, okay, what do we have to lose? Take Rosy along, he'll help you look."

But before Rosy could get off his chair, Buckley was out the door and heading for supply.

To everyone's amazement, he returned in less than an hour, a fuel control assembly tucked under one arm.

Sergeant Taft exclaimed, "Well, I'll be! I checked every bin over there," he said in a manner designed to eliminate any doubt Rosy and I might have of his thoroughness. He asked, "Where was this?"

Buckley seemed anxious to leave. "Oh, it was there, Sarge. See you guys … you too, sir," he said, and then scrambled out the door.

A few days later, Buckley once again performed his magic. This time he returned with a fuel transfer valve and an engine-driven generator, both for 260. And once again he acted in too much of a hurry to take Rosy along, or afterward explain anything to Sergeant Taft, who by then began to seriously doubt his own capability.

Sergeant Townley seemed quite pleased with Airman Buckley's new found talent and said, "Major Bensen might have something with that crazy theory of his."

Major Bensen didn't have any theories to help me out of one rather embarrassing situation. Every day the same airman from base supply came in, handed me the supply receipts to sign, and then Rosy hauled the parts to a special bin we had set up for 260.

The routine remained the same as always until one day after I signed the receipts, the airman asked, "Where do you want the fire truck, sir?"

"Fire truck?" I read the nametag on his fatigues and asked, "Shillings … what are you talking about?"

"You own a crash and rescue fire truck, Lieutenant. That's what you just signed for. It'll be here in a minute."

At that moment, I groaned as a gigantic, red, multi-million dollar fire truck pulled into the parking lot and proceeded to park alongside the hangar.

Sergeant Townley and the crew chief had access to 260 for three full weeks, a week longer than Major Bensen had promised. They found enough corroded fittings, ducts, cables, and valves to make the major shake his head until each of the corresponding parts were replaced or repaired on the other aircraft.

On the F-106, as with most jet aircraft, the flight control cables, rods and pulleys, are almost inaccessible, buried deep in a mess of electronic gear. Originating in the cockpit and going back, these critical parts of the flight control system can only be reached from the top of the fuselage during a complete tear-down inspection.

Sergeant Townley made his most significant discovery one day while Sergeant Taft and I visited 260 in the hangar to take inventory. I saw the sergeant on top of the fuselage, partially buried in a mass of control cables. The crew chief sat, perched like an Indian, ready to hand him any tool he requested.

As he forced a control cable back and forth, Townley exclaimed, "I got it! I got the son of a bitch."

The crew chief, trying to look into the confined area where the sergeant worked, asked, "What is it, Sarge?"

A few minutes later, Townley proudly displayed a flight control pulley he had extricated from the bowels of 260.

The crew chief examined the little pulley and said, "Looks pretty corroded."

"It sure is," said Townley. "It's a fiber pulley and the control cable could hardly move on it."

Not all aircraft have the fiber pulleys, but we did find four other aircraft with two each and two severely corroded fiber pulleys came out of an aircraft which had just been on alert.

I forwarded several of the pulleys to the depot for inspection. A report came back telling us it looked like salt induced corrosion. A subsequent report told us the manufacturer did not recommend them for use in a salty environment. I checked the aircraft records and found the birds with the fiber pulleys had all been assigned initially to a squadron in Michigan and later transferred to the Cape.

Major Bensen kept one of the corroded pulleys as a paperweight and sent another, along with my detailed report, to Colonel Wyler.

According to Janice (she wasn't sure whether he was looking at the pulley or at my report) the CO muttered, "What's this crap?"

The big day finally arrived, a bright, almost summer-like Friday in the middle of May and following five of the squadron's finest, Colonel Wyler blasted off in aircraft 381. A staff sergeant from the *Olefield Oiler*, the base weekly newspaper, and a master sergeant from *The Air Force Times* arrived early and waited at the squadron. Ten minutes later, at exactly ten-thirty, a base bus arrived, bringing the other members of the press. Captain Johnson and Sergeant Talifano greeted everyone. As expected, the small, local Cape papers also sent representatives.

Captain Johnson's most noteworthy catch, a tall, shapely blonde writer from the *Associated Press* in Boston, stepped off the bus last. Named Claudette, she had a high, afro hairdo, wore a short mini-skirt and looked braless. Sergeant Talifano looked excited as he escorted her, according to Captain Johnson's plan, to a front row seat in the operations' conference room.

Fortunately, Janice had typed a handout to provide some basic information on the squadron because Claudette's presence in the front row completely disrupted Captain Johnson's well-rehearsed speech. Janice said it included, among other things, a most complimentary synopsis of Colonel Wyler's career, but an abbreviated briefing resulted, leaving the colonel's career out. The group was taken to Hangar One for refreshments, prior to meeting the five selected pilots, scheduled to land at five minute intervals followed by the grand finale—Colonel Wyler in 381.

Once again, Hangar One had been miraculously converted into a showroom. Sergeant Paris and Airman Jones from the drag chute shop, provided the colorful banners hanging from the beams and walls. As a reward for patience and a job well done, Sergeant Townley selected 260 to stand on display in the center of the otherwise hollow hangar. Steps led up to a platform so anyone who wanted to could look into the cockpit. The crew chief stood by ready to soak up the prestige in his freshly laundered olive green fatigues. Several airmen manned a huge punch bowl and the base band tuned up outside the hangar.

It took the colonel and Captain Johnson just ten minutes to pick the five pilots for the momentous flight. Lieutenant Commander Buzz Thompson from the Navy, being handsome and photogenic, became the first pilot picked and would go off first. Lieutenant Holt epitomized the *fighter pilot spirit*, whatever that meant. Lieutenant Parks provided youth and vitality. Captain Seimons, the Air Force veteran offered experience, and as a bonus, Janice said the colonel mentioned that everyone would like him. She also said that Major Harmon, being somewhat overweight, became a slight problem, but as the colonel said, the Operations officer could not be slighted.

According to Janice, selecting the crew chief to park 381 turned out to be a much greater problem, although it shouldn't have been because 381 already had a perfectly able and willing crew chief in the person of Airman Panza. The complication began when the colonel asked Janice to get Talifano. In strict confidence, she related what happened after the sergeant entered the office: She overheard the colonel telling Talifano that Captain Johnson thought there needed to be a little more *color* for the ceremony. She said Talifano started to tell the colonel about the colorful ceremony being planned when the colonel interrupted and explained that Captain Johnson thought since we didn't have any black pilots in the squadron, maybe a black crew chief would be good for public relations. Janice said the first sergeant left the office muttering.

In all fairness to Sergeant Talifano I don't think anyone could have devised a more difficult task than trying to convince Sergeant Townley to switch crew chiefs in the name of public relations. But Talifano tried everything from reasoning with Townley to admitting that the colonel wanted a black crew chief.

Talifano put the matter before Major Bensen who considered the request for less than three seconds then said, "I wouldn't think of overruling my line chief."

Lieutenant Commander Thompson landed first and parked out on the line. As he walked to the open hangar the band broke into a rousing *Anchors Aweigh*. Buzz presented his clean, sparkling smile for the photographers, handed his gear to an airman then proceeded to the punch bowl to answer questions from the reporters and writers. Lieutenant Holt came down next and the attention shifted, except for Claudette from the Associated Press who stayed with Thompson. Then Captain Seimons came in and finally Major Harmon, but Claudette still stayed faithful to the Navy.

At last Captain Johnson directed the group's attention to 381 as it turned onto final approach. Commander Thompson and Claudette took good advantage of the diversion and slowly edged their way to the rear of the hangar. Then, only witnessed by myself and several admiring young airmen, they slid out the side door.

The colonel made a precise landing and within minutes taxied toward a special parking spot right in front of the hangar. Airman Panza proudly directed the colonel to the spot. I noticed Townley basking in glory, right up front with Talifano. When Panza gave the colonel the signal to cut the engine, Townley gave the big first sergeant a slight elbow right in the ribs to remind him of his victory in keeping the crew chief. Talifano stood stone-faced, refusing to acknowledge Townley's triumph. The colonel climbed down the ladder and the band went into *Wild Blue Yonder*. As he reached the bottom, flashbulbs exploded and the colonel posed with a big smile. Talifano smiled too, and I saw him direct Townley's attention to one slouching tuba player in the band. A cloak of pain spread over Townley's face as he recognized Airman Buckley.

That evening, I had an early dinner at the officers' club then settled down to watch television in the BOQ. Janice had already left with her parents for the weekend to visit some relatives. About eight thirty, Parks and another bachelor pilot, Lieutenant Frank Harris, rushed past the TV room then turned around and came in.

Parks asked, "Television … on a Friday night?"

I guess it seemed strange for someone to stay in on a Friday night. "What else? Janice went away for the weekend."

With a boyish squeak, Parks asked, "What else? Broads that's what else."

Harris rubbed his hands and said, "Yeah, come on, Joe. Tim Holt and Buzz got them all rounded up. The party's ready to start."

"What party?"

Parks explained, "A party to honor old Three-eighty-one (381), at Howard Johnson's in Falmouth. We got a suite."

Without moving a muscle, I said, "I don't know."

Parks pleaded, "Hey, come on, Joe. We'll teach you how to live a little. Besides, we might need a maintenance officer to keep us flying straight."

I gave in. "Well, okay. Give me a few minutes to get dressed."

Since joining the squadron, I heard about the bachelor pilots' parties. It seemed they never passed up an opportunity, no matter how remote. An automatic party developed whenever someone got promoted or transferred, and if one of the married pilots became a father, the bachelors celebrated. It didn't really matter if the father came or not, and as I recall, one new father didn't get informed.

A good rumor always resulted in a party and the pilots talked for weeks about the blast while the rumor spread that Colonel Wyler would be leaving the squadron. They had a party in honor of Captain Seimons the night he went back on flying status. The captain learned about it two days later, and I heard about a party in honor of the Russians—vodka only.

We drove to Falmouth in three separate cars. When we reached Howard Johnson's, Parks, like a hound on the trail of a fox, led the way up an outdoor stairway.

Tim Holt answered the door. "Hey, look who's here! Everybody cool it, maintenance is here," he joked as we entered.

They had what they called a suite, two adjoining rooms, each with a private bedroom. Besides Tim and Commander Thompson, I counted eight other pilots, not all of them bachelors, and at least twelve girls. I saw Cindy, the waitress from the officers' club, and Claudette, the blonde writer from the Associated Press. The others I never saw before.

Parks didn't waste any time. After fixing himself a drink he went straight to Cindy and asked her to dance. Frank found a tall redhead alone in one corner.

For awhile, I moved about, just trying to be friendly and got introduced to Claudette.

She said, "So you're a maintenance officer … how nice."

But before I could think of anything intelligent, I noticed she had very little on under a spacious knit dress and the words just tumbled out of my mouth, "Yeah … yeah, I'm in maintenance."

Rubbing her hand on my arm, she said, "Oh … that must be so interesting. We'll have to talk sometime."

"Sure … I'd love to."

Parks and Cindy came over holding hands and when he saw Claudette up close, he asked, "Dance?"

"I'd love to," Claudette replied and Parks, visibly shaking, handed me his drink, a double martini. He pulled Claudette real close and shut his eyes. Most of his head became buried in her afro and it looked so funny we all had a laugh. I saw Cindy snuggle up to Buzz so I drifted away and talked with a pretty little brunette, followed by an older blonde, then a girlfriend of Claudette's until a pilot asked her to dance and forgot to bring her back.

After a couple of hours, the group thinned out somewhat. A few of the pilots left with girls, but both bedrooms looked occupied. In one, I saw a married pilot having a serious discussion with the little brunette, whom I'd met earlier. Parks looked really out of it, curled up and sleeping in one of those pedestal chairs in a corner.

When the redhead Harris clung to all night went into the bathroom, he came over and sounded excited. "I got a real live one."

"How do you know?"

He looked insulted. "Are you kidding?"

"Where is she from?"

"The trailer park outside the base. Her husband's in Vietnam."

I asked in a whisper, "She's married?"

"Yeah, so is that little one you tried to make out with. Her old man's in the squadron … on the night shift, I think. No luck?"

"No," is all I could say with a lump in my throat.

The redhead exited the bathroom and asked, "Ready, Franky?"

Harris winked an eye and said, "Yeah, let's go. See you, Joe."

I fixed myself another drink. Buzz and Claudette danced and looked like a nice couple. With Parks sleeping like a baby, I noticed Cindy had herself another pilot.

When the record stopped playing, Claudette came to me and said, "Come on, let's talk about maintenance."

"Sure," I said.

We sat on the couch and Claudette curled up, her knees against my thigh. She had my undivided attention, We must have talked for over an hour because the next thing I knew the room looked almost empty. Lieutenant Commander Thompson sat patiently sipping a drink while Parks snored wildly in a corner.

Parks left his car in Falmouth that night and returned to the BOQ with me. I didn't see him at all on Saturday, but early Sunday morning, he burst into my room with The Boston Globe.

He asked, "Did you see this?"

"No."

A full-blown story appeared on page three, along with a big photo of Lieutenant Commander Thompson standing by his aircraft, the apron in the background.

I said, "Hey this is great."

"Yeah, but it looks like the Navy is running ADC."

I skipped through the article then said, "I know, but look at all this about maintenance. And look here … there's even a paragraph about Major Bensen."

"Wait till the colonel sees that," said Parks. "They didn't even mention him in the entire story."

"Yeah, that's too bad."

Chapter 8
The Accident

The rest of May turned out glorious with plenty of sunshine and nice warm weather through Memorial Day. At the end of the month, a feature story about the squadron and old 381 appeared in *The Air Force Times* and pleased Colonel Wyler. Janice described him as beaming over the story. The colonel had other reasons for being happy, too: The flying went well and with only the month of June remaining in the second quarter, it seemed certain we would surpass our flying quota and maybe even recoup the lost time from the disastrous first quarter.

On the first weekend in June, the colonel went to West Point for his class reunion, and when he returned on Monday, we had another commander's briefing. The big thing on the colonel's mind this time was the ORI, expected to come in July as soon as we returned from our week at the Air Force Weapons Training Center at Tyndall Air Force Base, Florida.

During the first full week in June, it rained, and I mean rained every minute of every day, right through the weekend. Janice said that sometimes it rained like that on the Cape in June, and we both felt sorry for the first wave of tourists coming for vacations.

The rain continued on Monday morning, and I joined Sergeant Townley in the pickup to watch the aircraft returning from the first launch. Townley had the vehicle pointed straight at the approach end of the runway and we waited for the first bird to appear between the slow moving wiper blades.

As a far away spot appeared in the distance, the sergeant said, "Here she comes."

We watched as the aircraft grew larger, taking form. The crew chief, draped in a black shiny rain suit, readied the spot.

The aircraft approached the base boundary then its rate of descent increased suddenly and Townley yelled, "What's he doing!"

We watched in disbelief as the aircraft approached, making headway but rapidly descending. Just when it seemed he would make it, the left wing struck the very top of a lone towering pine tree outside the base. The aircraft dropped, wings level and gear down, hitting the ground in an area of scrub brush. It bounced up, still moving forward, seeking the runway. We could see it come down again, wings still level, right on the highway that skirted the base. It continued along the ground and plowed into the heavy wire fence surrounding the base. The left wing dipped and the right wing flew up. In a blur, it flipped end over end then flipped again.

I grabbed the mike. "Control … this is Flight line one!"

"Control … here. Go ahead, Flight line."

The fire and rescue vehicles screamed by and the words wouldn't come out.

Control came back with, "Come in Flight line."

"Control … one of our aircraft just crashed!"

"What! Say again, Flight line!"

"An F-one-oh-six (106) has crashed!"

No reply.

Sergeant Townley put the pickup in gear and started for the crash site. Major Bensen came running out from Hangar One and waved so Townley made a circle. The major squeezed in next to me.

I asked, "Who is it?"

"Captain Seimons, in Two-fifty-one (251)."

Townley exclaimed, "Oh God!"

A dirt road led off the runway and took us to within a hundred yards of the crash. Sergeant Townley jumped out and ran ahead, tripping and falling several times. Already, cars lined the highway where the aircraft crossed, and the curious onlookers watched from inside their vehicles as the rain continued. The fire department had poured foam over the fuselage. I saw no signs of ground fire.

The major and I followed Townley to a group huddled around an inert form covered with an opened chute.

Tears poured down his cheeks as Townley said, "He's dead."

Feeling grief-stricken, I blurted out, "Oh no."

Major Bensen, soaking wet and shaken by the pronouncement, covered his face with both hands and stumbled away.

Soon afterward, they removed the body and more and more people arrived at the site. General Braddock came with two second lieutenant aides and proceeded through the wreckage strewn area. A second truckload of air policemen arrived, and I listened to Captain Lickle caution the officer in charge to make sure that nothing got touched or disturbed. Major Bensen and Townley walked slowly through the wreckage, giving pause each time one of our aircraft approached on a cross runway.

Colonel Wyler and Major Harmon, also part of the same launch as Captain Seimons, had not yet arrived.

I joined the major and Townley once again as they walked back across the highway to the point of initial contact, the lone towering pine amidst the scrub brush. "I think he would have made it if he hadn't hit that," Townley said, pointing to the top of the broken tree.

We traced the flight from that point: After hitting the tree, the aircraft dropped quickly, hitting the ground hard and leaving two deep tire imprints in the rain soaked earth. Then it bounced, just as Townley and I had witnessed, touching down again on the highway.

Fortunately, there had been no traffic. The left tire hit the highway curbing, breaking off the left gear, the only part of the aircraft left outside the base. With the left strut off, the left wing dipped and the right wing flew up as the aircraft sailed into the wire fence. Caught in the fence, the left wing separated clean at the fuselage line. The aircraft flipped and landed upside down, crushing and ripping the tail section and canopy. The right wing separated and the battered but momentum-filled fuselage, flipped again, throwing out Captain Seimons, surely already dead. After landing right side up, the fuselage continued sliding to its final resting place, leaving a mowed path cluttered with torn and separated parts.

When the colonel and Major Harmon arrived, the rain had slowed to a drizzle. The colonel went directly to the battered fuselage where General Braddock and the aides looked at the aircraft. I followed behind Major Bensen and Townley. The fuselage, covered with foam and ripped open, had gaping holes in the black synthetic fuel cells.

Colonel Wyler and the general looked at the crushed engine and one of his aides, a young second lieutenant, remarked, "General, there's no fuel left in any of these cells."

General Braddock checked, looking down, then straight at Colonel Wyler he said. "You're right."

The colonel shook his head. "Can't be. I just can't imagine an experienced pilot like Captain Seimons running low on fuel."

Major Harmon agreed, "Not a chance."

His comment seemed to irritate the general.

Major Bensen asked Townley, "Did you see any fuel around, Sarge?"

"It's hard to tell, sir. There are traces of fuel on the leaves, a greasy residue, but the ground's too wet to tell anything. The bird flipped. The fuel could have been thrown out. Look at the size of those holes. That cell there is completely shredded," he said, pointing at a big hole in a fuel cell.

Major Bensen said, "That's what I think. When the aircraft flipped, the remaining fuel could have been thrown out."

Major Harmon spoke up, "I agree. A lot of the fuel could have atomized before reaching the ground."

Colonel Wyler said, "It looks like engine failure to me."

General Braddock spoke in what I thought seemed a sarcastic tone. "We'll see. Let's find out what the tower knows."

Sergeant Townley dropped Major Bensen and me at the base control tower. Colonel Wyler, Major Harmon, and Captain Lickle arrived at the same time. General Braddock and his aides, already inside, listened as a nervous looking chief master sergeant told what he knew.

The sergeant explained, "It was a perfectly normal flight, sir, until the flameout call."

The general demanded, "Let's hear the recording."

"Yes, sir."

We huddled around to listen. First we heard a lot of background noise then Captain Seimons's voice. "Emergency … flameout!"

The controller's voice shrieked, "What! Say again, Scarecrow!"

Loud and clear for the last time the captain calmly repeated, "Emergency, flameout!"

The tower sergeant then said, "That's all, sir. I rushed to the window and saw the bird approaching. At first it looked normal. It was almost home. Then the wing hit that tall tree," he said, looking out the window.

The rest of the story correlated with what we had pieced together at the site.

Colonel Wyler said, "Sounds like he lost power on final."

General Braddock asked, "Were there any fuel calls?"

"No, sir."

Major Harmon spoke, "It couldn't be that. The flight was only a little over an hour long. I had plenty of fuel when I got down."

Colonel Wyler nodded in agreement.

The general asked, "When does the investigation team arrive?"

Captain Lickle answered, "First thing in the morning, sir."

"I want one of my aides there to follow the progress."

"Yes, sir," said Captain Lickle.

The accident investigation team arrived early and sat drinking coffee in the mess as Major Bensen and I entered. I saw the team had a full bird colonel in charge. The others included an F-106 pilot, a medical officer, a maintenance officer, a chief master sergeant, and several other officers and airmen.

As we ate, Captain Lickle came over to the table and asked Major Bensen if it would be all right if I served as the coordinator for the team. The major gave his permission and as soon as everyone finished eating, I followed Captain Lickle to the pilot's conference room for the preliminary briefing.

Captain Lickle outlined every known detail of the accident. The team members listened intently, taking notes as he spoke. The colonel in charge took the forms and records of 251, which I had packed in a box, and immediately passed the box to the team's maintenance officer. Near the end of his briefing, Captain Lickle introduced me and informed the members that I would provide any needed supplies or equipment. Then he introduced several squadron airmen who would serve as chauffeurs. Airman Buckley sat ready to do anything.

The captain turned the floor over to the colonel in charge, a tall, stern looking man who exuded efficiency. "Well, gentlemen, you heard the details," he said. "Now we have a job to do. All of you have been on investigations before, so I won't waste time going over procedures. At the end of each day we meet on the second floor, the room right above this conference room. And as in all investigations, we go day by day, until we find the cause of the accident." Then he seemed to boast as he said, "I haven't been on an investigation yet that couldn't be solved." He turned to Captain Lickle. "Captain, we're going to be interviewing a lot of squadron personnel so I want it understood that our purpose here is to find the cause of the accident for one and only one reason … to prevent any further accidents. We're not here to fix blame or find fault, so I'll expect everyone's cooperation."

"Yes, sir," Captain Lickle responded.

The colonel concluded, "Okay, gentlemen, that's it. Before we go to the site, give the lieutenant here a list of anything you'll need."

Just about every one of the inspectors requested something, and after the last had left for the site, I pondered my list, wondering where to begin. They requested one pair of medium size coveralls, a 100 foot tape, graph paper, several notebooks, different colored tags, a box of envelopes, a pair of dividers, a magnifying glass, one flashlight, containers for fuel, oil, and hydraulic fluid samples (although there would be no fuel samples), a package of Reynolds Wrap, and a complete set of parts catalogs. The maintenance officer also wanted a dentist's mirror.

I wondered, *Why didn't they bring some of their own stuff?*

For some reason, I thought about the silly, little maintenance kit my friends at Chanute had given me. I wondered if this is what they tried to tell me.

I decided to start with the envelopes and climbed the stairs to see Janice. She kept typing as she held a wet hanky in one hand then stopped, pulled the letter from the typewriter and handed it to me:

Dear Mrs. Seimons:

It is with the deepest personal feeling that I attempt to express to you the profound sense of loss existing in this squadron as a result of the death of your husband, Joe.

> Since joining the squadron Joe has earned a place in the hearts of the officers and airmen with whom he has served. His pleasing personality and devotion to his comrades made his presence always appreciated. His absence will be most noticeable.

I stopped reading because tears also filled my eyes and blurred my vision. I thought about Captain Seimons and how he always helped me, and how everyone loved and respected him.

Colonel Wyler's letter explained the facts of the fateful flight and concluded:

> No final conclusions can be reached from so little positive information, but the Air Force is presently conducting a complete and exhaustive investigation. As additional facts are developed you may be assured that I will inform you immediately.
>
> I would like you to feel that it will always be a privilege to perform any service I can for you. Please communicate with me or any member of my squadron if we can be of assistance to you.
>
> With deepest regrets,
>
> Colonel Wyler

I spent the entire day rounding up supplies and delivering them to the second floor office. I found most of the items in the squadron, but I did have to make one trip to Falmouth for the Reynolds Wrap and dentist mirror.

The next morning we returned from a sad funeral to find the investigation in high gear. Almost immediately, the team realized the cause of the accident would not be readily apparent and finding it would require a thorough, painstaking investigation of every little detail. According to Air Force regulations, they had two weeks to complete their study and submit a preliminary report.

Because of the *flameout* call, everyone suspected engine failure. The dirt covered power plant had been taken to Hangar Three where it sat on a platform near the engine shop. After studying the badly damaged power plant for a full day, the team's chief master sergeant reported he could find nothing which would have caused the engine to fail. So that evening, we carefully loaded the engine on a flatbed and shipped it to the depot for a detailed teardown inspection.

A review of the aircraft records also failed to furnish any leads and for days I escorted the investigators to the various maintenance shops. All the squadron personnel cooperated, but one could sense the apprehension as the inspectors checked various parts for proper operation, while at the same time, asking probing questions about maintenance procedures and practices. Any parts or mechanism, which could not be tested or operated without causing damage, went to the base hospital to be x-rayed. But the inspection of all the individual parts and systems failed to uncover anything more.

Over the weekend the team decided to use Hangar One to reconstruct the aircraft parts and systems in their respective positions. Sergeant Townley had the airmen clear one half of the hangar for the endeavor and he placed 381, with all its panels removed, in the other half to serve as a reference. The remaining parts from the crash site got placed in the hangar. We hung chicken wire forms to set up the vertical pieces. The wings and tail section sat, precariously balanced on scaffolds, and then fitted against the battered fuselage, until the ghost of 251 became recognizable.

When they assembled the wreckage parts in their final place, we discovered the spear like pitot boom from the nose still missing. Sergeant Townley and I returned to the crash site and found the pitot boom half buried in an area several hundred feet ahead of the fuselage imprint. It must have been launched like a spear.

On Monday morning, the specter of 251 sat for all to see as the team attempted to find a cause. I saw several investigators trying to match individual strands of wire from the same control cable, but by midweek they still had not found anything significant.

The next day, the report on the engine returned from the depot, confirmed the master sergeant's earlier findings and dashed the hopes of the investigation team. I sensed their frustration and even overheard one member suggest that maybe Captain Seimons had been under the influence of alcohol. The medical officer quickly pointed out that his examination revealed no sign of alcohol or other substance that could have affected the captain's performance. He further indicated that interviews with the crew chief, the last person to see Captain Seimons alive, and Mabel Seimons, attested to the fact that the captain had been in good spirits, looking forward to completing a successful career before enjoying his retirement and grandchildren.

That same day, at the request of General Braddock's aide, the same second lieutenant who thought he discovered the absence of fuel, the team held a closed door meeting. Afterwards, I heard several team members talking about the unsubstantiated theory that Captain Seimons had run out of fuel. That rumor spread throughout the squadron in a flash.

Shortly afterward Airman Tiddyings, an instrument technician, came to me with a frightened and guilty look. "Lieutenant, I have something you should know about," he said, "and I want to tell the accident investigation team too."

"What is it?"

Tiddyings said, "There's a lot of talk about Captain Seimons running out of fuel, and I think I had something to do with that."

Then he began to cry.

"Now wait a minute. Before you start blaming yourself for anything, tell me about it."

He regained his composure a little and started to explain: "When Two-fifty-one (251) was undergoing a periodic inspection the fuel calibration tester didn't work right, so I sent it to the depot for repair, but I still signed-off that I had completed the test on Two-fifty-one (251)."

"What exactly does the test do?"

"Well, it's a check to verify that the fuel gauge reading in the cockpit is accurate and coincides with the amount of fuel that's actually in the tanks."

"I see ... but the PE inspection on Two-fifty-one (251) was completed months ago."

"Yes, sir, but what if the fuel reading happened to be off all that time?"

"I just don't know," I had to admit. "Have you told Warrant Officer Shock?"

"No, sir."

"Well, maybe we should discuss it with him and Major Bensen."

I located the major then he called Warrant Officer Will Shock and Sergeant Townley. We all met in his office.

Airman Tiddyings related the story once again.

Major Bensen said, "Well, I think you can rest at ease. That PE is ancient history and Two-fifty-one (251) flew a lot of sorties since then. The crew chief or one of the pilots would have surely discovered any discrepancy by now."

Will said, "That's for certain."

But Tiddyings still had the same concerned look on his face.

Townley got up from his seat and headed for the door as he said, "I'll be right back."

Major Bensen asked, "Where are you going?"

"Maintenance control. I need to check something."

A few minutes later Townley returned, carrying the log book from maintenance control. "I think this does it for certain," he said while opening the book to a date back in March.

Will inquired, "What do you have there, Sarge?"

Townley asked, "Remember when Two-eighty (280) busted the strut? Well, the colonel told Captain Lickle to call the birds still in the air to have the pilots burn off all excess fuel before landing."

The major exclaimed, "Sure, that's right!"

"Here it is," Townley said, pointing to the log for that particular flight. "Two-fifty-one (251) flew that flight, and I'm sure the pilot took that fuel needle down to nothing before he came in."

Major Bensen added, "And it occurred right after the periodic inspection."

Relief came to Airman Tiddyings' face. He paused for a few seconds then said, "I still think the inspectors should know about it."

Warrant Officer Shock spoke up, "Don't be ridiculous. What's the sense of bringing something like that up now?"

"Wait a minute, Will," said Major Bensen. "Airman Tiddyings is right. The team should know about this. I'm sure after they've had a chance to look at everything and talk to the pilot who flew Two-fifty-one (251) that day, they'll agree with us."

I notified the team's maintenance officer and Airman Tiddyings, this time completely at ease, retold his story. Then we located the pilot who flew 251 on the flight when all the excess fuel had to be burned off.

He exclaimed, with a vivid memory, "You better believe it! I kicked in the afterburner until that baby flew light as a feather. That gauge read correct or they'd still be looking for me in the dump."

That afternoon, Sergeant Townley and I received notification to appear at the final hearing in the morning as eyewitnesses to the crash. Airman Tiddyings also received his notification.

On Saturday morning, the team listened to all the testimony and in the afternoon they completed their report then departed.

The long Fourth of July weekend seemed forever and when we returned on Tuesday morning, Janice showed me a copy of the report left for Colonel Wyler. It looked to be a half inch thick so I quickly scanned the pages until I reached the final conclusion:

> After a careful and detailed analysis of all factors involved, it is the opinion of the investigating board that pilot error, system malfunction, or material failure were not contributing factors. The only possible contributing factor found was maintenance malpractice in not having completed a fuel system calibration test.

Every member of the investigation team signed the report.

At lunch I saw Major Bensen cringe as Captain Lickle showed the report to several curious pilots. Later in the afternoon, I watched a detail of airmen haul the parts of 251 to a wooded area alongside Hangar Four.

One airman asked, "Was it really maintenance malpractice?"

Sergeant Townley declared, "Hell, no!"

An airman with a puzzled look on his face then asked, "Well then … what happened, Sarge?"

Frustration in his voice, Townley answered, "The answer's still buried in this rubble."

Chapter 9

The Black Sheep

With the investigation complete, and the cause of the accident undetermined, but left to conjecture, an indescribable pall soon developed and hung over the squadron. To the inexperienced maintenance man and for most of the pilots, it probably seemed like nothing more than an uneasy feeling, but to others like Sergeant Townley and Major Bensen, I sensed something much more profound. Perhaps a frightful suspicion that whatever made 251 crash, also lurked in the rest of the aircraft, growing like a cancer.

Major Bensen told me he had another frightening concern, the effect the unfounded accusation might have on young Airman Tiddyings. I heard him tell Warrant Officer Shock to watch Tiddyings very closely and report any sign of trouble.

For a few days, Colonel Wyler remained silent. He finally expressed his feelings by ordering maintenance to provide one aircraft each morning for Captain Lickle's thorough inspection. Janice told me that as far as she knew, Major Bensen didn't try to talk the CO out of his decision which seemed like an accusation of maintenance. She said he once walked slowly out of the colonel's office, looking very disappointed.

In the days following the investigators departure, something needed to happen to dispel the gloom in the squadron. Unaware, relief came with the arrival of two pilots from the 69th Fighter Interceptor Squadron in Michigan. They walked through the door in supply, one carrying a large box and the other lugging two empty orange crates, one in each hand.

The one with the box declared, "She's all yours, Lieutenant."

I had just lost a bout with the base supply officer who refused to take back the fire truck because of some complicated technicality I couldn't understand, so I feared what might be in store for me as I asked, "What do I own now?"

He had a smirk on his face, placed the box on my desk and said, "Old Fifty-five. These are the forms."

He explained that aircraft 255 was a replacement from the 69th for 251, and then I felt much better when I learned I didn't have to sign for the aircraft.

When they left, Rosy told me that while I talked to the one, the other pilot (the one with the orange crates) inquired as to where they could pick up a load of live lobsters.

Rosy explained, "He said they're having their squadron picnic this afternoon and they wanted to take back lobsters."

I asked, "How are they going to get them back?"

As if the answer should have been obvious, Rosy declared, "In the orange crates."

"I know that, but where will they put the crates?"

"Hey, you got a point there, Lieutenant. Anyway, I sent them to Captain Hogan's Fish Market in Buzzard's Bay."

I pulled the latest forms for 255 out of the box and took them to Sergeant Townley. The sergeant already had people looking at the new bird. I saw a swarm of maintenance personnel at the new aircraft. Airman Bean, the former crew chief of 251, had been assigned to the new aircraft, and Townley gave him instructions to remove the 69th insignia from the tail section and put up the scarecrow emblem.

I said, "I see we have a replacement already."

Townley said,"Yeah, I got the shops out here to take a quick look at her before we accept the bird."

"Do we have a choice?"

"Sure, but once the colonel signs the release, she's ours, so I want to make sure everything's okay before those pilots leave."

Next to 255, sat the other 69th aircraft, a two-seat B-model, in which both pilots would return to Michigan. It surprised me to see Airman Buckley servicing the aircraft.

I asked, "Airman Buckley's handling aircraft now?"

"Yep," Townley said then admitted it wasn't entirely voluntary on Buckley's part. "We get a lot of transients in the summer so he has to."

Remembering the real reason I came out to the line, I asked, "Say, how are they going to get those lobsters back?"

Townley said, "Would you believe the armament bay?"

"No!"

"Yep, come over here, Lieutenant, you have to see this."

I followed the sergeant under the aircraft. All the connectors and wires in the weapons bay had been carefully wrapped and tucked out of the way to prevent any damage.

I declared, "Well, I'll be … pretty clever."

"Yeah, and if Captain Roberts ever saw this, I think he'd faint."

Within an hour, Sergeant Townley had a good idea of what to expect from the new aircraft.

After reviewing the report from some of his radar technicians, Will Shock advised, "That radar couldn't find a B-52 if it crawled up its tail."

Sergeant Singly from the engine shop added, "Man, I can't believe that engine got that bird here."

An airman from the hydraulic shop sighed and said, "The fluid is contaminated … bad."

So there would be no doubt in Townley's mind, Airman Bean, who inherited the new bird, summed it up: "She's a real pig, Sarge!"

The transient pilots returned from Captain Hogan's just before lunch with their crates (four in all) filled with big red lobsters crawling in green, slimy seaweed. They left the crates at the aircraft with Airman Buckley, giving him instructions to guard them till after lunch, when they would depart.

During lunch, Major Bensen turned to the next table where the colonel and Major Harmon sat with the two pilots from the 69th and said, "Colonel, maintenance doesn't accept 255."

"What? That's ridiculous. Why not?"

"It's a mess. Send it back."

Looking stunned and embarrassed by the major's audacity in front of the two visiting pilots, the colonel said, "Nonsense, Harry. We need that bird. We're keeping it. Get it ready."

I heard that Captain Roberts learned of the unusual use of the armament bay from one of his technicians, but to insure that he would not become an accomplice, he avoided the aircraft and even decided to skip lunch, fearful that someone might mention it and implicate him.

After lunch, Airman Buckley helped load the crates into the armament bay. Shortly after, Buckley guided the F-106B out and the pilots departed.

Several hours later, the time it would take for the aircraft to reach Michigan, Janice received a call from an enraged Colonel Breathstone, the commander of the 69th Fighter Interceptor Squadron. She said that Colonel Wyler had not returned from his flight yet, so she took Breathstone's message as best she could, considering that he yelled very loud. She said that Breathstone explained that when the aircraft reached the 69th and the armament door opened, they found the large red lobsters cooked to the size of little green shrimp and enmeshed in burnt and brittle seaweed. She said that Breathstone, obviously very upset, felt that someone at the 50th must have thrown the switch for *full heat* in the armament bay and the pilots flew to Michigan without noticing. Breathstone told Janice he would wait for Colonel Wyler's phone call.

Janice told Colonel Wyler and said the colonel roared like a lion, started laughing then rushed and told Major Harmon, but completely ignored Colonel Breathstone's request for a return call.

The next morning Breathstone tried again to reach the colonel and Janice had to tell him that the colonel and Major Harmon went golfing. I guess Breathstone couldn't take it anymore because in less than two hours he landed at Olefield, asking directions to the golf course.

Airman Buckley parked Colonel Breathstone's aircraft and gave him detailed directions. When Buckley entered the flight line lounge, he said the colonel's teeth looked clenched and the veins in his neck swollen out like hot hydraulic lines. A group of curious airmen decided to follow behind the goliath 69th colonel.

When they returned the story got told: According to Sergeant Conn, who heard it from one of the flight chiefs, who related what one of his more reliable crew chiefs had told him, Breathstone waited patiently at the clubhouse until the colonel and Major Harmon walked onto the ninth green, a picturesque water hole. Then to the bewilderment of the two golfers, Breathstone strode onto the green, walked between them to their carts and commenced throwing the colonel's clubs, one by one, into the center of the lake. He then bent the colonel's cart over one of his massive legs and threw that into the lake.

The story did not sound entirely consistent throughout the squadron. In the flight line lounge, I listened to one crew chief describe how ridiculous Colonel Wyler looked, crawling out of the lake. Then in the mess, I listened as Lieutenant Holt mimicked Major Harmon, struggling for his life in the lake. The pilots roared, encouraging Holt.

After that episode, everyone found it a little easier to get back to the business of maintenance. Sergeant Townley and Airman Bean set out to work the bugs out of 255, which each day proved itself more of a maverick. Almost every day, Bean came in supply to order parts or check with Rosy on the parts already on order.

One day, Rosy took longer than usual to research a part number so Bean asserted himself and said, "Come on, Rosy, get a move on."

Rosy asked, "What's your hurry? Afraid those electronic boys are messing up your bird?"

Bean answered, "No, I got them trained. Besides, they're not too bad," he admitted to my surprise.

"Well then," Rosy said, "hold your pants on. The lieutenant here can't afford to own another fire truck if I make a mistake."

"Right," I agreed. "Besides, we like having a celebrity around," I added, bringing a smile to Bean's face.

It didn't take long for the new bird to get nicknamed the *Black Sheep*, and according to plan, Sergeant Townley and Bean went about the task of getting the new aircraft ready so Major Bensen could release it to Operations.

For a while, the CO seemed tolerant of the aircraft being out of commission and let maintenance work on the bird. But then he became his impatient self and began calling Sergeant Conn for a daily status report. Finally, his curiosity got the best of him and he ventured into the hangar to see the aircraft first hand. Quite by coincidence, Major Bensen and I entered the same hangar and saw the colonel talking to Bean.

We walked quietly (quite a feat for Major Bensen) over to the aircraft, right behind the CO and the major said, "If you want to know the status of an aircraft, I'm the chief of maintenance."

The colonel jumped. “Well … well, you’ve had this aircraft for a week and a half,” he stammered. “I think it’s time it flew.”

The major said, “Soon”

“How soon?”

“Oh, four more days should do it.”

The colonel ordered, “That’s too long. Make it two.”

Referring to Captain Lickle’s daily inspections, the major said, “It would have been ready a lot sooner if your inspector didn’t tie everybody up with a lot of unnecessary work.”

From what I heard in the squadron, the inspections failed to turn up anything more significant than frayed lines and a few loose connections, and Captain Lickle frequently pulled an airman off a job to get an opinion when he thought he found something.

After the colonel left, Sergeant Townley came to the aircraft and asked, “Any luck calling off Captain Lickle?”

The major said, “No, but maybe we can do something about it.”

“I’m willing to try anything,” Townley offered. “If he did any good it would be okay, but there’s more important work to do than all the crap he finds.”

“Yeah, I know,” Major Bensen said, “so starting tomorrow on this bird, and every other aircraft, have the crew chiefs point out popped rivets to Captain Lickle.”

Townley gave the major an incredulous look and asked, “Every popped rivet?”

He then gave Major Bensen a look like he wasn’t sure whose side the major was on.

Major Bensen calmly replied, “That’s right … every single one.”

After Major Bensen walked away, Townley muttered, “He’s mad … the sheet metal shop will never be the same again. Wait till Jonsey hears about this … he’s mad.”

Sergeant Harold Jones, the NCO in the sheet metal shop, had a cheerful disposition and hailed from Mississippi. I stopped in the shop in the afternoon and got a clue to the major’s *madness*. Sergeant Jones had been assigned a new project—building a new golf cart for the colonel. He hadn’t started construction yet, but I watched as he put the final touches on a full-size sketch, which he had neatly taped on the wall.

In his distinctive drawl, he asked, "Like it, Lieutenant?"

I said, "Yeah, pretty sophisticated for a golf cart."

Jones beamed. "Nothing but the best for the CO. The colonel gave me the go ahead today."

Not letting on that I knew there might be other plans for his talents, I said, "Great."

Before Sergeant Jones cut the first piece of metal for the new golf cart, Sergeant Conn sent over a work order to repair forty-nine popped rivets on 375. Following Sergeant Townley's instructions, Airman Harkins, the crew chief of 415, pointed out all ninety-eight popped rivets to an astonished, but quite pleased Captain Lickle.

Janice told me that the captain rushed into the colonel's office with his report.

She said the colonel congratulated the proud flight safety officer, telling him to keep up the good work.

After more aircraft reports and about a thousand more rivets to repair, Sergeant Jones estimated that at Captain Lickle's rate it would take eight months, three weeks, and two days for his shop to complete their work, if they worked weekends and holidays. And to insure that all progress ceased on the golf cart while Jones had rivets to fix, Major Bensen put the sheet metal shop on his daily itinerary.

For a while, Jones managed to avoid contact with the colonel, but finally faced the CO and explained the reason for the delay.

The next day Captain Lickle delivered his inspection report for aircraft 400. Prior to the captain's inspection the aircraft had been sitting in Hangar Four, the armament area, for three consecutive days, and in addition to the usual discrepancies, Lickle had discovered a bird's nest in the left wheel well. Janice told me that Captain Lickle seemed quite proud of his find and had asked her to place it on the colonel's desk along with his report.

Without explaining, the colonel told Captain Lickle aircraft 400 would be the last of his inspections. Janice said Captain Lickle seemed puzzled and said he only completed half the fleet.

Later that same afternoon I overheard Major Bensen telling Sergeant Jones not to refer to an Air Force captain as a bird dog. Jones just smiled and went on his way.

Chapter 10

A Maintenance Solo

One week before the squadron's scheduled trip to Tyndall Air Force Base, Florida, I got a pleasant surprise from Major Bensen. I would be going as the maintenance officer in charge.

With disbelief, I exclaimed, "Me!"

"Sure. Don't you want to go?"

I replied, "Yes, sir ... but I never expected to be *in* charge."

The major assured me. "Well, it's the best way to learn."

When I told Janice, she seemed impressed then she laughed and said, "I've known for several days now, Joe. At first Colonel Wyler insisted that Major Bensen go. The colonel said we're sure to get the ORI as soon as it's over, and he said he really wanted Major Bensen down there."

"And?"

"The major convinced him that you could handle everything as the maintenance officer down there." She then added, "He said if you couldn't go then nobody would."

"I see."

Everyone really looked forward to the trip. The pilots seemed especially anxious because in addition to learning the latest tactics, the training included firing live rockets at towed targets. For maintenance, the week would be a test of our ability to support operations and maintain the birds to meet the flying schedule. And as the colonel said, "It was the final opportunity before the Operational Readiness Inspection."

I felt more reassured when I learned that Sergeant Townley had also agreed to make the trip, and the sergeant showed me the preparations he made. All the supplies and equipment for the week sat ready on the side of Hangar One. Sergeant Taft and Rosy had packed several crates with the spare parts Townley requested. Somehow, the parts Sergeant Taft listed as not available, Airman

Buckley managed to come up with just before they nailed down the crates and attached the manifests.

The roster of maintenance personnel included the best in the squadron, all handpicked by Sergeant Townley.

Everything waited on the apron as the two C-123s appeared on the horizon then slowly landed. Minutes later the two big cargo carriers groaned to a halt on the apron and the loading took place. A shiny, but ancient C-54 landed and Sergeant Townley checked off the names of the men as they boarded.

Major Bensen and a group of airmen waved goodbye as the C-54 taxied for the runway.

Sergeant Townley and I sat in the first seat right behind the cabin. The ride started out bumpy in the old prop and the airmen made a lot of noise. The crew chiefs from A-Flight and the radar technicians seemed to be getting along fine, even sitting together. Townley noticed it too, and looked a little suspicious when he saw Airman Bean playing a game of chess with one of the technicians. It sounded funny because after each air pocket we could hear Bean, apparently gaining an advantage as he reset the fallen chess pieces.

Half an hour later, the radar technician declared, "Checkmate!"

Bean cursed and promised several on-looking crew chiefs that next time he would do better.

On the last leg of the flight, Townley and I got into a little discussion about airplanes. The sergeant had known so many different birds since World War II and all seemed to be indelibly stamped in his memory. He didn't mind escorting me through the annals of military aviation.

Before we landed at Tyndall, I asked, "What kind of legacy do you think the old F-One-oh-six (F-106) is going to leave, Sarge?"

He replied, "The *Six* is writing new history every time she goes up. If someone told me ten or even five years ago that a high powered jet would log seven thousand hours on active duty, why I'd tell him he was crazy, it's not possible."

I added, "Some of the old props sure have a lot of durability."

Townley explained, "There's a big difference between a prop and a jet. A jet engine imposes a lot of stress on an airframe. As a matter of fact, the engine stresses the hell out of itself."

I guess we both sensed that the discussion seemed to be leading back to the fateful accident, so we both settled back in our seats and rested as the silvery C-54 made its descent into Tyndall.

At Tyndall, we set up shop in a huge maintenance hangar right near our assigned runway. A little Quonset hut on the side served as our maintenance office. Half the aircraft arrived Sunday afternoon and flying began early the next morning. The schedule got hectic, starting early each day and flying until mid afternoon with quick turnarounds, simulating actual battle conditions; then we worked late into the night to get the birds ready for the next day.

Sergeant Townley and the other NCOs made all the important maintenance decisions. I didn't have much to do except give my support and show genuine interest and concern. I did have to call back to Olefield and brief Major Bensen after each day's activities. Colonel Wyler insisted on a daily rundown.

In the middle of the week, the first nine birds returned to the squadron on the Cape and our other nine interceptors landed at Tyndall, led by Colonel Wyler in 381.

On Friday afternoon, our final day, the old *Six* once again gave us real cause for concern. The first indication of trouble came as usual, when the ominous crash and rescue vehicles, lights flashing, rushed toward our assigned runway. Within seconds, a crowd of airmen gathered around our truck.

The call came over loud and clear. "Scarecrow Squadron, this is Tyndall Operations."

Grabbing the mike and sounding apprehensive, Townley said, "Go ahead Tyndall Ops."

"One of your birds is coming in hot, with a fire. The pilot is going to try bringing her in."

Townley ordered, "Bean, Kelly, Clymer, get a jack and a ladder. Come on, you guys, hustle!" The airmen threw the equipment in the rear of the pickup and jumped in. With his head out the window, he said, "Clymer, get a tractor and a tow bar ready too."

Airman Clymer jumped out and the sergeant pulled away.

Soon, I saw the aircraft coming, black smoke trailing behind.

Airman Bean yelled from the back of the pickup, "Looks like a fuel fire, Sarge."

Townley nodded as the aircraft came closer and the black cloud grew large, partially enveloping the fuselage.

Even before we could pick off the tail number, Townley said, "It's Three-hundred (300)."

I checked the clipboard and announced, "Lieutenant Holt."

Scratching his head, Townley said, "Lieutenant Holt … well, we always knew he had more guts than brains."

The cloud of smoke enlarged more and Townley added, "Good luck, kid!"

We reached a position midway down the runway and to the side on the grass. The fire and rescue vehicles pulled up a little further down. Aircraft 300 touched down very hard and began rolling toward us, black ugly smoke billowing around the fuselage. Holt held the nose up for aerodynamic braking and the smoke looked intense as the bird went by then screeched to a stop forward of our position.

We watched as Holt unbuckled and Townley muttered, "Get out of there, kid, before she blows."

Just then, Airman Bean rushed by the window, carrying an aircraft ladder over his head.

Townley screamed, "No, Bean … don't!"

But Airman Bean had made up his mind and rushed without hesitation to the smoldering aircraft. He set the ladder as Holt ripped off the last strap. Holt climbed down and he and Bean ran from the aircraft as two fire trucks pulled up, one on each side of the aircraft. They began smothering the bird with foam.

After the firemen got the fire under control, Townley sighed, "That was close."

That evening we learned just how lucky Lieutenant Holt and Airman Bean had been: An engine bleed-air duct failed, dumping 600°F air on an engine-driven generator, which failed from the heat. Townley showed me where the shaft failed at a spot other than the necked-down shear section. This permitted continued rotation and the abnormal heat generated by the rotor rubbing against the stator ignited a nearby fuel line. The sergeant said Lieutenant Holt and Airman Bean had luck going for them because the entire fuel system could have exploded.

No one would have questioned Lieutenant Holt if he had aimed the aircraft out to sea and bailed out. For saving the bird he eventually received an Air Force Commendation for Bravery. Later that month, Airman Bean received the Crew Chief of the Month award without going before the NCO committee then got selected as the Squadron Airman of the Month.

We worked well into the evening, digging into 300 to evaluate the damage. Other than me, Townley and two other NCOs remained. Townley let the airmen leave for a little celebration party on the last night at one of the local beaches. Earlier, several airmen picked up a load of hot dogs and beer, and from the talk I overheard all day on the line, most of them had dates with girls they managed to meet during the busy week.

We finally decided to call it a day and as I fumbled with the lock on the hut door, an air police station wagon pulled up.

A young AP lieutenant inquired from the vehicle, "Lieutenant Harrington?"

I answered, "Here."

"Good," he said. "I'd like to inform you that the Panama City police have locked up one of your airmen."

Looking tired after our long day, Townley said, "Oh, no."

I asked, "Who is it?"

"Airman Parkinson," said the AP officer. "I don't know all the details, but they called us and said they went to break up a noisy party down at the beach because some of the locals complained. To make a long story short, they said they just wanted to break up the party, but this one airman got cocky and they had to put it to him."

Leaning against a wagon, Townley asked, "What's the charge?"

The lieutenant said, "Are you ready … disturbing the peace and drunk and disorderly."

Townley and I exclaimed in unison, "What!"

With a grimace, the lieutenant added, "He resisted arrest too."

"Christ! That's ridiculous," Townley uttered. "Why didn't somebody call us first?"

"Like I said, they just wanted to cool things off, but Parkinson gave them a hard time."

Then Townley admitted, “Well, he can be a hothead, but he’s a damn good crew chief too.”

The lieutenant, said, “You’ve been informed. It’s all yours now.”

As the vehicle drove away, Townley said, “You have to do something, Lieutenant. If we go back home without Parkinson, sure as hell the colonel will court-martial him.”

Feeling utterly helpless, I said, “I know, but what can I do now?”

Townley lamented, “If only Major Bensen were here.”

His words felt like a dagger, giving me a stabbing reminder of my responsibility.

Against his wishes, I dropped Townley off at the barracks and headed straight for the Panama City police station. By the time I found the place I felt ashamed of my earlier hesitation and on the way, I became determined to do whatever necessary, short of a jail break, to free Airman Parkinson.

As I entered his office, I saw the sheriff of Panama City. He looked large and had a face like a punch-drunk fighter and arms like ham hocks. He surveyed my grimy flight suit and scuffed boots with what looked like a gleam of admiration. Then, quite routinely, he started to read the arresting officer’s report. In a way, it even sounded a little complimentary because the airmen willingly broke up the party and the arresting officer noted that ‘the airmen seemed cooperative’. But then the sheriff got to the part where Airman Parkinson threw an empty beer can, hitting one of the policemen on the head.

In a raspy voice the sheriff said, “I don’t like anybody throwing things at my people.”

I nodded, agreeing wholeheartedly.

He dropped the report on his desk and looked at me. “Well?”

I found out then I wouldn’t have made a good lawyer because I fumbled terribly. Then I got on the right track, describing the grueling week at Tyndall and telling him how hard Airman Parkinson worked all week.

I concluded with, “We’re leaving tomorrow, and I hope we can take him with us.”

The sheriff seemed unmoved so, more out of desperation than anything else, I said, “We have a line chief who’s dying to get his hands on him.”

With renewed interest, the sheriff asked, "Oh yeah, what's he like?"

I related a story, concocting a personality, part Townley, part Talifano, but mostly a figment of my imagination about a hard-nosed World War II veteran.

When the sheriff interrupted to tell me about his own war experiences, I had the suspicion he might release Parkinson and drop the charges, which he did, but only after I endured his war story.

I listened to him describe his time as an infantryman on Anzio Beach. He told me that his company had lain for thirty-four days and nights in shallow, grave-like trenches as the Germans shelled their position, how they had bailed water out of the trenches with canteens and how after two weeks, scabs began to grow between their legs. He grabbed his bulky chin and shook it to show me how his teeth rattled as the shells exploded around their position.

Early the next morning, we arrived on the line to check all the bleed-air ducts before the birds departed for home, but aircraft 300 had to stay at Tyndall for repair. In addition to the fire damage, the hard landing busted the engine mounts and wrinkled the fuselage skin.

As the C-54 lifted off, Townley remarked, "Jonsey's going to be glad he doesn't have to repair Three-hundred (300)."

Airman Parkinson slept like a baby, curled up in the last seat and before we got halfway home, I came to appreciate the wisdom of the sheriff's decision to release the young airman. Townley had a few ideas that sounded infinitely more constructive than a jail cell or a court-martial.

During the final leg of the flight, I slumped back in my seat and Townley, looking out the window, asked, "Got any big plans for tonight, Lieutenant?"

"No, nothing earthshaking," I said. "Janice and I are just going to take in a movie over at Hyannis."

"My wife and I, and another couple, are going over to the NCO club. I'd like to have you join us, if you could?"

That invitation had a traumatic effect on my nervous system, but somehow I managed to restrain myself.

I finally got it out, "Well, uh … uh … why sure, Sarge."

"Good. We'll meet you and Janice in the lobby of the club, about eight."

"Okay."

"You two are kind of going steady with each other, huh?"

I admitted, "Yes, I guess you might call it that. Nothing serious, but we date."

"Well, she's a good-looker. Nice girl too. Say, I just thought of something. The club has a stripper tonight. Is that all right?"

"No problem," I said, unsure of what Janice might say, but knowing for sure we wouldn't tell her father.

For the balance of the flight, I kept quiet, but my mind seemed like a whirlwind. I recalled telling Janice how Major Bensen felt about me getting invited to the NCO club, and I couldn't wait to tell her the news. As for the major, I imagined the expression on his face as he learned that Townley had invited me to the club.

For a moment, I feared I had misunderstood Major Bensen. What if his comment that first day happened to be nothing more than a silly joke? I tried to remember how many drinks he had that night in the officers' club, but I couldn't recall.

My heart sank and I had to consider what I knew of Major Bensen, and I recalled our first discussion when he said, "People are a maintenance officer's job, Joe. Only people make the difference."

The words rattled around in my head as I struggled to remember everything since that first day. One thing for sure, Major Bensen always demonstrated unusual faith in the airmen and NCOs in the squadron. People didn't get *led* in the customary military fashion; instead they received help, guidance, and above all, trust. For a military man in a position of authority, he had a unique style of leadership. Major Bensen never used formal or top-down authority to motivate the men; instead, he used a *bottom-up* approach which required *acceptance* from the airmen and NCOs.

The answer hit me. For an aspiring maintenance officer, getting invited to the NCO club had a lot of significance, and I realized then that Major Bensen knew the NCOs would never invite an officer to their club without due consideration. I also realized being invited by the line chief had to be extra special.

On that final leg of the trip home, the significance of Tyndall dawned on me: It happened to be my *solo* as a maintenance officer, and I knew I made it.

Janice looked stunning in a short, pale blue evening gown and her father said very little while I waited, but as we left he remarked, "Pretty snazzy for a movie in Hyannis."

Janice smiled and I waved goodbye.

We arrived at the NCO club fifteen minutes before eight. Like most other facilities on base, it had been an Army barracks and looked pretty drab on the outside, except for a brightly colored canopy at the center entrance. Inside, it looked a lot different, plush as any topnotch nightclub.

Sergeant Townley and his petite wife Susan, arrived at eight sharp. The sergeant looked like Joe College in a white turtleneck and blue blazer. Susan, an attractive brunette with an outgoing personality, remembered me from the children's Christmas party. Janice and Susan became instant friends.

We found our table, up front near a raised stage in the large dining area with plenty of room for dancing on either side.

Within minutes, the other NCO, Chief Master Sergeant Nobel Sterling, a tall thin master sergeant with a manicured mustache, and also a line chief in the SAC squadron on base, arrived with his wife, Margaret, a plump cheerful woman. She seemed unaffected by two, protruding teeth that caused a slight whistle as she spoke which seemed to be a lot. Sergeant Townley managed to get a few words in, showering me with praise on the Florida trip and Janice looked impressed.

Both NCOs ordered steak and the rest of us selected the house specialty, boneless breast of chicken. As we ate and enjoyed the music of a bouncy trio, I noticed several other squadron NCOs with their wives and friends. Sergeant Conn and Sergeant Jones sat at a nearby table and when Townley waved and got Jones's attention, the sheet metal NCO rushed to our table and praised our judgment for leaving aircraft 300 at Tyndall.

Townley laughed, giving me the credit without telling Jones we didn't really have any choice.

I couldn't believe it when I saw the unmistakable Talifano at a table in the rear. I guess I never expected to see the spit and polish first sergeant in a Hawaiian shirt and actually having a good time. I wished I could have taken a picture to show the crew chiefs.

For some selfish reason, I wanted Talifano to know that I came as a guest of Townley so I excused myself and conveniently walked by his table. As I passed, I tapped his shoulder and said, "Hi, Sarge, nice to see you."

Slightly inebriated, he shouted, "Hey, Lieutenant! How you doing?"

"Fine, Sarge. You look like you're having a good time."

"Yeah, who you with?"

"Janice and Sergeant Townley."

"Hey, that's right, you and old grease head just got back from Florida. How'd it go?"

"Real well, Sarge. How's everything at the squadron?"

"Good. Everything on campus is good. Now that Tyndall's out of the way, the colonel expects an ORI."

"Any day or night now, I guess."

"Yeah."

Then, he said, "Hey, wait till you see this broad tonight."

His wife gave him an elbow in the ribs.

Without thinking, I asked, "Oh, you've seen her before?"

My question seemed to add to her displeasure.

Then with a lingering sigh, Talifano said, "Yeah, last night. Bet you wouldn't kick her out of bed, Lieutenant."

Everyone laughed except his wife, who became furious.

I started to walk away and said, "It should be interesting."

Talifano beckoned me back then asked, "Say, Lieutenant, did you hear about that airman … the one from the instrument shop that didn't complete the fuel calibration test?"

"Tiddyings?"

"Yeah, that's him."

"No, what happened?"

Talifano said, "Yesterday we had to take him to the VA hospital in Boston. The kid flaked-out. Remember how quiet he got after the investigation? Well, all of a sudden last week, he started acting real crazy … smashed the TV set in the barracks … claimed that somebody was watching him through the tube. He kept talking about religion and believe it or not … Christmas tree ornaments."

I muttered, "Oh my God."

"Yeah, that's what Major Bensen said."

I went to the men's room, and it took awhile for me to regain my composure. I decided for the time being to keep the news from Townley.

During our first dance, Janice said, "I see Sergeant Talifano told you."

"Yeah, I wonder how Major Bensen feels."

Supporting Major Bensen she said, "Bad. He blames that stupid investigation team. He told the colonel if it's the last thing he does in the Air Force, he'll find the real cause of the accident."

"What did Colonel Wyler say?"

"He warned him not to touch the wreck. He said Airman Tiddyings is in good hands now that he's receiving psychiatric treatment. Why can't we check the crashed aircraft?"

I explained, "It's against Air Force regulations. Aircraft Two-fifty-one (251) doesn't belong to us anymore. Pretty soon we'll be getting disposition orders to ship it to some depot."

After our dance, a loud drum roll summoned an NCO in uniform to the stage. He announced, "And now, ladies and gentlemen … for your gourmet pleasure, straight from New York City, may I present, Miss Lady Godiva."

The room filled with catcalls and whistles then Lady Godiva, a tall, Amazon-like redhead, attired in a tight black, leather cowgirl outfit, emerged from the rear and proceeded to wiggle her way through the crowd. As she climbed the stage amidst the incessant howls, Janice took my hand and gave it a squeeze. Several NCOs lifted a large, horse-like structure, upholstered in red velvet, to the stage. The house grew silent, all eyes glued to the stage as Lady Godiva began her first routine. Wiggling and writhing, she moved on the stage for ten minutes, slowly removing clothing until she was down to only a G-string and tasseled pasties.

When she moved to the velvet horse, Janice squeezed my hand. The grand finale took another breathtaking fifteen minutes of undulation on the soft velvet then ended abruptly with Miss Godiva still wearing the G-string but only one of her pasties.

The ladies applauded politely, but the NCOs started shouting, “More … more … more!”

As the tempo increased, more NCOs joined the chant.

The screams came from all sides, “Take it off! Take it all off!”

Sergeants Townley and Sterling managed to refrain, but both thoroughly enjoyed the other NCOs.

A familiar voice screamed from our side, “Come on Red! Just like last night!”

I looked and saw Sergeant Talifano, right up front.

Miss Godiva jumped off the stage, smiling, throwing kisses, and pushed through the crowd. I watched as Talifano followed close behind the scantily clad stripper until an arm reached out and yanked the big first sergeant into his seat. Then I saw his wife.

Townley enjoyed the whole spectacle and said, “Remind me to bring you over here some Friday, Lieutenant. That’s stag night.”

But on the way home, I had to promise Janice that I would forget about Sergeant Townley’s offer.

Chapter 11

Silver Chum

As I entered my cubicle in supply on Monday morning, Major Bensen called me on the phone.

I listened briefly and said, "Yes, sir, I'll be right over."

Without taking his nose out of a supply manual, Rosy chirped, "Must be pretty important."

I knew it too, because Major Bensen never asked anyone to come to his office for routine matters. He went to them.

As I walked into his office, he looked fresh from his morning tour of the line and said, "Grab a chair, Joe."

We talked for some time about the week at Tyndall and it pleased me that he seemed satisfied. I suspected that Sergeant Townley had put in a good word. Then he came to the reason he asked me to come over.

Smiling, he said, "Joe, I think you're ready to be our flight line maintenance officer. How about it? Are you ready?"

I exclaimed, "You bet Major!"

"Good, it's yours. I know you'll do a good job."

With some trepidation, I said, "I hope so, sir."

He reassured me. Well, I know how you feel, Joe. It's a big responsibility ... the toughest job in maintenance. Just remember a few basics and you'll do fine."

I nodded.

Then he said in a serious tone, "Take care of your airmen, Joe. Always remember that each man is unique and needs the opportunity to do his thing ... something he can do better than anybody else."

Thinking of a young airman, the one becoming the best scrounge Sergeant Townley ever knew, I asked, "Like Airman Buckley?"

"Right, like Buckley," the major said. "An airman comes into the Air Force with certain attitudes and skills, Joe. It's up to us to provide the right environment so he can flourish and contribute.

Don't get me wrong, I'm not against discipline. There's a place for that too, but too often it's used to suppress natural ability."

"I think I know what you mean, sir."

Then, passing on the wisdom of his experience, he continued, "Good. There's something else that's important too … be a generalist … not a specialist. Heaven knows, the Air Force has enough technical specialists. So don't try to be a better technician than your airmen. That's their job. The NCOs know more about the nuts and bolts of an aircraft than you and I could ever hope to learn. But it's our job and responsibility to know them, their needs, their hopes, what's buggin' 'em. Be sensitive to those things and they'll take care of the airplanes, I promise you.

He rose from his chair and we walked to the door, his arm around my shoulders. "Joe, I almost forgot to tell you. I talked to Sergeant Townley this morning on the line. He wants to take a look at Two-fifty-one (251). I told him to go ahead."

"Isn't that against Air Force regulations?"

His teeth looked clenched around his pipe and he said, "Yes, but that's not important right now. We have to find out why that bird crashed. Townley's convinced the answer is still somewhere in that heap of junk."

"Do you think so?"

"I don't know. I hope so for Tiddying's sake. It's not too late yet. The head shrinkers can play all the games they want, but that kid needs to be convinced."

"Yeah, I guess so."

"The other thing I want to tell you, Joe, is that it's going to get awfully hectic around here. We'll be doing a lot of flying, among other things."

"How come?"

The major replied, "Someone in ADC told the colonel that we're in for an ORI this month. He's going to push hard to get ready. Should be like gangbusters … I guess you're too young to remember gangbusters, huh?"

"Yes, sir, but I thought that's why we went to Tyndall."

"Yeah, it is. The colonel is overreacting, but his mind is made up. This is his first ORI, and he's determined to impress ADC."

Major Bensen made my responsibilities clear. That morning, I bade farewell to everyone in supply and records then moved to the flight line on the opposite side of Hangar One.

As I left, Rosy said, "We must have trained you pretty good, Lieutenant."

It surprised me to find Sergeant Townley had prepared for my arrival. He had my office floor waxed and the desk dusted off and polished. A new sign on the door read: "LT. HARRINGTON—FLIGHT LINE."

As Major Bensen had warned, the next several weeks seemed like gangbusters. Every day in August we flew like crazy, pounding the birds for all they could take. Since the nuclear load would be such a critical part of the ORI, the colonel had no qualms about putting the *Sunday Punch* into affect a lot. He initiated it frequently and at the most unexpected times—like four in the morning or right after a shift change. The weekends seemed like his favorite time and everybody always rushed in because we didn't know if it would be another drill, the start of the ORI, or heaven forbid, the real thing—the Russians.

The routine never changed. First the foreboding procession of nuclear weapons from the storage site then all the operationally ready birds got loaded while Captain Roberts checked and rechecked the loading procedures. After the load, the *live* weapons went back to the storage site and the flying commenced.

I could see the fatigue on the faces of the airmen, but Colonel Wyler felt it necessary to push them: "In order to hone the squadron into a true fighting machine."

Janice said that on more than one occasion she heard Major Bensen objecting, but the colonel said he wanted to be sure we would be ready for anything an ADC inspection team threw at us.

After one especially bitter confrontation between Colonel Wyler and Major Bensen, she said she suspected the colonel's motives when she overheard the colonel say, "There's a lot of bird colonels sitting on their ass in ADC that would love to get this command. They never did like someone from SAC moving in on them."

The *Sunday Punches* occurred so frequently, and at all kinds of weird times, they caused more than a few problems in the squadron, understandable when considering that a lot of the airmen relied on outside jobs, and the alerts threatened to alter an ADC lifestyle—moonlighting.

On the flight line alone, I discovered we had six auto mechanics, three bartenders, two tourist guides, a maitre d', two life guards, a bait shop proprietor, his helper and three NCOs who established a thriving business selling clams and lobsters on the Cape. I wondered how many I didn't know about.

Sergeant Townley and I managed to resolve most of the conflicts amicably, always keeping in mind the interests of the United States Air Force, but a few situations did get a little out of hand. One morning the recall went operational at four a.m. and everyone in maintenance rushed in, but the pilots and Colonel Wyler never showed up. Major Bensen got upset and called the colonel at home. The colonel's wife answered and informed him that the colonel, still asleep, had not initiated the recall. The major's mouth fell open.

He remained that way for a few seconds then politely asked, "Would you please awaken Sleeping Beauty?"

The colonel denied initiating the recall and Major Benson looked more confused.

After hanging up, he said, "It sure sounded like the colonel's voice. My phone rang and I picked it up. The colonel, or somebody else, I guess, declared *Sunday Punch* and hung up. It sure sounded like him."

Half of the airmen accused the colonel of being underhanded and the other half, like Airman Bean, figured Major Bensen must've had a terrible nightmare. Not long after, Sergeant Townley reported that one of the airmen admitted calling and initiating the recall, absolving Major Bensen.

Townley became suspicious when Airman Fritz, who had a reputation for being quite proficient at voice imitations, didn't report in for the recall. After questioning, Fritz quickly confessed that he had called the major, declared *Sunday Punch* then hung up.

When I talked to Fritz, he said. "I couldn't sleep, Lieutenant. I haven't been able to sleep nights ever since the alerts started."

I learned that Airman Fritz had been working at the squadron from four in the afternoon until midnight then in the mornings and on the weekends at a gasoline station just outside the base, or he did until his employer fired him for sleeping on the job.

Sergeant Townley seemed sincerely sympathetic, but to be sure that Fritz realized the gravity of his act, the sergeant moved him to the day shift temporarily and assigned him the distasteful job of crawling up tailpipes to inspect the turbine blades for cracks.

His first day on the new job caused quite a stir. According to Janice, the colonel looked out his window as Fritz emerged from the tail of one of the aircraft on the line.

She said, "The colonel screamed for Sergeant Talifano. Then I heard a loud crash in Talifano's office and ran into the hall. I saw the first sergeant in his doorway, sprawled over his waste paper basket and dripping with coffee like a tackle recovering from a block. He then jumped up and rushed past me into the colonel's office and snapped to attention and he said, 'Yes, sir! You called, sir?' The colonel then asked him, 'What on god's earth is that cloud of dust walking on the line?' Still at attention, Talifano asked, 'Cloud of dust, sir?' and the colonel said, 'get over here'. Talifano said, 'Yes sir.'"

Sergeant Townley and I happened to be in the opened hangar and we saw the first sergeant running out on the apron. Fortunately, Fritz had already entered the tailpipe of the next aircraft. I saw some crew chiefs laughing as Talifano frantically searched the line for the soot covered airman, and when he inquired, the crew chiefs only shrugged their shoulders. Meanwhile, Fritz, having been warned of the hot pursuit, remained buried deep in the tail of 415.

When Townley stopped laughing, he said, "We need to do that more often."

Another situation, involving Tech Sergeant Cummings, the robust and likable flight chief of the squadron's T- Birds, became no such laughing matter and gave us all a few sleepless nights. Cummings happened to be our bait shop owner and his business enterprise became exposed one Saturday morning when the colonel called another one of his surprise alerts. We had completed the nuclear load and the birds had just taken off. Townley and I returned to the lounge and found Talifano waiting for us with two very serious faced fishermen.

Leaving the two in our custody, Talifano announced, "These two gentlemen need to see Sergeant Cummings."

Townley sent a crew chief to get Cummings.

I saw the same worried look on both bearded faces and asked, "Is there some problem?"

The shorter of the two fishermen answered, "If we don't get some silver chum this morning, we're in bad shape."

Completely at a loss I asked, "Silver chum?"

"Yeah, Sergeant Cummings is the only one on the Cape who sells it, Captain," the tall fisherman said—promoting me.

The other quickly added, "We waited over an hour for the shop to open. Then we called the sergeant's home and his wife told us about the alert. Is it serious?"

"No, it's just a drill."

Townley said, "This silver chum that Sergeant Cummings sells, what does it look like?"

The short fisherman said, "Just slivers and scraps of shiny metal. Here, I got some right here in my pocket."

He pulled out a handful of ECM (electronic countermeasure) chaff, the stuff our T-Birds dropped when they flew as targets, trying to confuse the Dart's radar during an intercept.

I saw the blood drain from Sergeant Townley's face. Cummings walked through the door as Townley examined the chaff in his hand. I had never seen an NCO cry, but at that moment, I think Sergeant Cummings nearly did.

Sergeant Taft in supply had a complete record of all the chaff that Cummings ordered and received. We figured that he sold about the same amount in the last three months as the T-Birds actually used during that same time as targets, and when confronted by the facts, Cummings confessed.

Sergeant Cummings had a bait shop business and sold the chaff in brown paper bags labeled as Silver Chum.

He explained, "I stumbled on the idea by accident one day while doing a little fishing for blues. I didn't have much luck with conventional methods so as an experiment, I threw in a few handfuls of chaff and within seconds the water boiled with big blues."

Sergeant Taft in supply didn't seem too concerned about all the extra chaff that Cummings had ordered and said, "To tell you the truth, Lieutenant, I didn't even know what we used that stuff for. Sure, I knew they dropped it from the T-Birds, but for all I knew, we could have been dropping it on the Russian trawlers."

When I told him, Townley moaned and said, "Don't get me wrong, Lieutenant, I think Taft is a great supply sergeant, but when it comes to—"

I interrupted, "I know, Sarge."

Sergeant Townley told me a little about Cummings. Everyone liked the T-Bird NCO and he had the reputation of being a hard worker, thoroughly dependable. He had three children and as Townley put it, "One in the hangar."

I asked, "What's your recommendation?"

Looking glum, Townley said, "He's an NCO in the US Air Force. That's a big responsibility, and he knew he did wrong."

I knew what he tried to say and asked, "Court-martial?"

"Yes, sir."

I wrote it up and presented it to Major Bensen, biting my lower lip as he read.

He said, "You did the right thing, Joe. There's no other way."

Military justice has often been compared to a speeding bullet, quick and deadly. Such was the plan for the court-martial of Technical Sergeant Alfred R. Cummings, AF 62125-6810. The Judge Advocate's office received the papers on Wednesday with a trial scheduled for Monday morning. Cummings resigned himself to take whatever he got.

The rest of the week became a painful, confusing experience for me. The troops on the flight line acted cool and suspicious, treating me like a traitor. The colonel reacted positively.

With Major Bensen present, he said to me, "It's gratifying to know we have someone in maintenance who appreciates the importance of discipline."

Only Major Bensen seemed reassuring. "I know what you're going through. It's the only thing you could do."

When I walked into my office earlier than usual on Friday morning, I surprised Sergeant Townley, who ducked something behind his back and tried to leave the office unchallenged.

I demanded, "Let's see it."

"It's nothing, Lieutenant, just some tools the night shift left by mistake. I'll make sure they keep out of your office from now on."

Blocking the doorway, I said, "Let's see it, Sarge."

Townley seemed reluctant as he produced a red brick.

"Some tool."

As he scurried out he said, "Yeah, I'll have to spend more time with that night shift."

I turned the brick over and saw the inscription—TRAITOR.

Before we quit, a T-Bird crew chief who worked for Sergeant Cummings, knocked on my open door and entered.

He snapped to attention and announced, "Airman Swartz, sir!"

"At ease, Swartz. What can I do for you?"

"It's about Sergeant Cummings, sir."

"Yes?"

"Well, sir, I was wondering. What if someone else was using the Silver Chum … I mean chaff, sir?"

Fully anticipating another confession, I asked, "What do you mean, Swartz?"

"I've been talking to some of the other guys, sir, and they said if someone was using the chaff, they'd be just as guilty as Sergeant Cummings, right?"

I tried to explain. "It depends, Swartz. If they knew they were using stolen Air Force property then sure."

"That's what the guys thought, too, Lieutenant."

"So?"

Swartz then revealed, "Well, sir, for two Saturdays in a row, General Braddock bought five bags of the chaff, sir."

Startled, I asked, "General Braddock?"

"Yes, sir. He has a boat, the Molly Bee, at the Falmouth marina, and he comes into the shop with his two daughters."

"How do you know?"

Looking nervous, he said, "During the past month, I've been working for Sergeant Cummings in the shop on Saturday, sir."

"Are you sure it's the general?"

"Yes, sir. There's one thing, though."

"What's that?"

Sounding doubtful, Swartz said, "I don't think he realizes that the Silver Chum is ECM chaff, sir."

"I'd like to see him explain that," I said, bringing a smile to his face for the first time.

The wheels began turning in my head faster than I could think. "Is there any more of the chaff in the shop?"

"Yes, sir … there's plenty."

"Good. Okay, Swartz, now listen carefully. Here's what we're going to do."

We arrived at the Falmouth marina bright and early Saturday morning. The little shop did a lively business. Surrounded by bags of Silver Chum in a tiny back room, I listened as Swartz politely explained again and again to fishermen.

"Sorry, we're temporarily out of Silver Chum. A new supply is due in any day."

While waiting with the bags of chaff, I saw the sign Swartz prepared, a beautiful four-by-four painted piece of plywood which read: Special End of Season Sale on Silver Chum. Today Only.

We waited patiently, but with no sign of the general. The Molly Bee sat swaying in her slip. Just as we thought about giving up, a big station wagon pulled into the parking lot.

From the front Swartz exclaimed, "It's him, Lieutenant. It's the general."

I looked through a small opening and saw the general wearing a yachting cap, a flower print shirt, white pants and old sneakers.

Swartz and I hauled the brown bags into the sales area and put the sign on top of the pile of bags then Swartz remarked, "Hot looking daughters, huh, Lieutenant?"

Crouched in the back room I said, "Yeah."

To our chagrin, the general and his daughters went to the Molly Bee, and after about ten minutes, we heard the large inboards start.

I moaned, "He's not coming in."

Before the Molly Bee got underway, Swartz rushed outside and started hammering the sign to the side of the shack.

The commotion attracted one of the general's pretty teenage daughters and she yelled, "Daddy, look! They're selling that special stuff … on sale, too!"

A few minutes later, the general and his daughters walked in the shop and started negotiating. I had to gasp as I heard Swartz refuse what I considered a reasonable offer for stolen Air Force property. The general made a higher offer and Swartz closed the deal, selling the entire supply.

I remained out of sight while Swartz, the general, and his two daughters loaded the bags on the stern of the Molly Bee, and as the boat pulled out, Swartz used my Polaroid to snap some beautiful, but incriminating pictures—one in particular showing the general and his daughters proudly posing beside the bags of Silver Chum.

Major Bensen took care of the rest rather quickly. A lieutenant whom I knew in the Judge Advocate's office told me that the major waited as they opened the office on Monday morning. That same morning, Sergeant Cummings, somewhat confused but happy, returned to the squadron and informed everybody that the charges against him got dropped.

Janice said Colonel Wyler was beside himself when he learned the court-martial was dismissed and said he called Talifano to ask him what happened. But Talifano didn't know anything except that Major Bensen went there. Janice said Major Bensen just smiled when the colonel asked him, and the colonel swore he would see General Braddock to get to the bottom of everything.

Through it all, Sergeant Townley remained convinced that 251 still held a secret and somehow he managed to find time to conduct his personal investigation. Every day he visited the roped off area alongside Hangar Four dismantling suspected parts and testing them. I couldn't argue with those who said he seemed obsessed.

Sergeant Fox in the electrical shop told me, "Townley's going to have to get me some new test equipment before he's through." I also overheard a young technician who watched Townley come and go past his hangar, say to another tech, "Those guys in the white suits will have themselves a chief master sergeant pretty soon."

The comments didn't deter the sergeant much.

Even Janice got into the act when a directive came ordering us to get a flatbed and ship 251 to the depot. She sent a copy to Major Bensen, but conveniently misfiled the colonel's copy.

As it turned out, Sergeant Townley's effort seemed to be in vain because he uncovered nothing new at the time. One day I noticed a lot of aircraft components with green tags attached stored in one corner of the flight line hangar, indicating the sergeant had tagged them as good and operable.

To make matters worse, during the month, two of our sister squadrons, the 69th in Michigan and the 41st in South Carolina experienced fatalities and both accidents appeared to be similar to the crash of 251, occurring at the last moments on final approach; the only difference being that in both cases the aircraft had not flipped like 251 and they still had plenty of fuel so it made us more certain that Captain Seimons didn't run out of fuel.

We heard rumors that quickly faded—the Air Force considered grounding the entire F-106 fleet.

Townley said, "What could they do? Reactivate the mothballed One-oh-twos (102s)? Now wouldn't that be some can of worms?"

We were fortunate in one respect, flying as we did all through the month, the birds held up well.

But that didn't impress Sergeant Townley and he warned us. "That's the way it goes sometimes, but if it ever turns the other way, look out!"

The aircraft performed so well that it became difficult for Major Bensen to convince Colonel Wyler that we were pushing our luck with the old *Six*.

As the flight line officer, Townley convinced me that we needed to get more time to perform normal preventive maintenance.

Sergeant Townley proclaimed, "It's stupid. You can't get away from preventive maintenance with an old bird like this."

The sergeant constantly reminded Major Bensen, even to the point of irritating him.

Major Bensen said, "I know, Sarge, and I agree, and I'm trying."

Sounding like a half apology, Townley said, "Well, okay, sir, I'm sorry. I guess it's open season on scarecrows this year."

Major Bensen really tried, but he couldn't convince Colonel Wyler to slow down. And I think every airman in the squadron knew why. The ORI would be the colonel's final exam, and it could either be a first step on his way to general or the end of any further progression, which, of course, would mean some obscure desk job to make room for the next aspirant. That seemed to be a brutal fact of life in ADC.

Then Rosy provided the simple idea that evaded so many others. I went back to supply to check on the status of a needed part. When Major Bensen walked into supply and Rosy, somehow unaware of the major's presence, kept complaining about all the alert drills.

He asked Sergeant Taft, "Why do we have to come into supply every time there's an alert? There's nothing we can do in here. Besides, all it would take is one good act of sabotage and the squadron would be wiped out."

At the mention of sabotage, I saw the major look in Rosy's direction for a few moments then he turned around and approached me, saying, "Joe, we're going over to see the colonel now, and this time we're going to get Sergeant Townley the time he needs to look closely at a bird."

We headed toward operations and I could only think of how our last effort with Colonel Wyler resulted in failure with Janice sitting there listening.

This time, the major approached the colonel casually, talking optimistically about our readiness for the ORI, saying "The birds look good. The radars are holding up just fine. The nuclear loads are like clockwork. I think we're ready in *almost* every respect."

Taking the bait, the colonel asked, "Almost? What do you mean by *almost*?"

The major replied, "We haven't checked out our security yet."

"Sabotage! I never thought about that!"

Major Bensen said, "It's pretty important, Colonel. The ORI team will probably try—"

The colonel interrupted, "I know, I know. But what can we do?"

"We've been so busy with alerts, and flying, and maintenance … if I had the time, I'd check out our security."

"That can be arranged." Then the colonel asked, "Why didn't you say something before?"

"I guess I wasn't listening," replied the major.

"What's that? What do you mean?"

"Oh, it doesn't matter. Good day, Colonel."

Chapter 12

Security Security

Everybody in maintenance knew Major Bensen would keep his word about checking out the security, but I couldn't find anybody who could think of what more should be done because the squadron already had an excellent record in such matters. To bring myself up-to-date, I checked with Captain Johnson, who maintained the records and information on security incidents. He showed me the files, a chronological incident history which included statements and even pictures of the intruders. It surprised me to learn the airmen on the flight line led in the apprehension of intruders above all other groups combined. Not that intruders posed any threat to the squadron, on the contrary, most looked like unsuspecting civilians or tradesmen who inadvertently entered one of the restricted areas.

The incidents mostly involved someone coming on base to visit a friend or relative at base housing. But then they got lost and ended up at the squadron. It surprised me to see that once at the squadron area, the civilians seemed to display amazing courage, completely ignoring the warning signs and wandering into the restricted zones. The squadron had detailed records of each incident, and since the reward for apprehending an intruder included a three-day pass, the airmen kept alert—I guess even anxious—to pounce on some unsuspecting prey. According to the records, they provided precise directions while always being polite, before asking their shocked victims to spread-eagle on the pavement until the air police arrived.

I looked at quite an assortment of pictures, but among the more noteworthy, I saw two rather helpless grandmother types, face down on the pavement, a cultured MIT physics professor, still smoking his pipe in the prone position and a smiling group of six local brownie troop members with their somewhat perplexed, but well endowed, blonde troop leader.

I discovered that Airman Buckley led the squadron in the number of captures, having apprehended six intruders in the past two years, and this explained the six notches etched in his seldom used tool box.

So it didn't come as a complete surprise when Major Bensen decided to start by taking a closer look at the security provided by the base air police detachment, responsible for guarding the alert cells at all times, and the squadron areas at night and on weekends. The major openly admitted the APs, being professionals, had the training to be quite proficient at the business of security. He said their motivation and dedication is what concerned him.

He also said, "If they screw up, it's still our ass."

The major got his first idea one day as we ate lunch. He announced he would entertain any suggestions for cracking the security of the APs.

Captain Roberts winced at the mere thought of anyone being able to get at the nuclear weapons.

Will provided an idea. "Why not penetrate the alert cells?"

Looking amused, the major asked, "How?"

Will replied, "It might be easier than you think. Just crawl under the eye."

The major said, "You're kidding, of course."

"No, I'm dead serious. That's a sophisticated electronic system and unless somebody's been carefully maintaining it, I'm sure it's out of calibration."

Will then gave us a very technical explanation of the system, at the same time convincing the major that it might be worth a try.

Major Bensen uttered, "Wouldn't that be something?"

The next evening, a dark, moonless night, I accompanied him to the apron near the alert cells. Across the eye, still quite a distance away, we could see several air policemen patrolling the well lighted alert barn. To the left of the cells, an AP guard sat, sipping coffee in the little guard shack that controlled the only road access.

"Well, here goes," the major said as he began to shimmy across the protected area on his stomach. Then a wide smile spread on his face as his elevated posterior passed the midpoint. When safely across, he stood up and whispered, "Unbelievable. Okay, Joe it's your turn."

I got on my stomach and snaked across, also undetected. We moved slowly toward the right side of the barn, keeping a safe distance in the darkness. A solitary AP patrolled the area, and when he turned the corner, we headed for the side door. But about ten feet from the door, I kicked an empty soda can and it went crashing against the thin, metal wall.

The AP came running around the corner with his gun pointed and ordered, “Halt! Don’t move or I’ll shoot.”

We froze and he played his flashlight on us.

He looked surprised, but also relieved and exclaimed, “Major Bensen! Did you come through the gate, sir?”

Handing me the soda can as if it were something I should save and cherish, the major answered, “No.”

“No, sir?”

“That’s right.”

“Well, are you authorized to be here, sir?”

“No.”

“Well, uh, I’m sorry, sir, but I’ll have to notify Captain Barry.”

“I understand. It’s quite all right. Besides, we have something else to tell the good captain.”

Captain Barry, the head of the base air police, arrived while the major and I drank a coke alongside the alert barn. The AP had a coke too, but when he spotted the captain’s wagon at the gate, he quickly discarded the can.

The captain jumped from his vehicle and said, “Airman, why aren’t these two on the pavement?”

“It’s Major Bensen, sir.”

The captain yelled, “I don’t care if it’s the President of the United States! You know your orders.” Then he reprimanded the airman. “I’ll take care of you later.”

Major Bensen defended the airman, “He did his job. He should get a three-day pass, not a chewing out.”

Sounding sarcastic, the AP captain replied, “We don’t reward people for doing what they’re supposed to do. Now, do you mind telling me what you’re doing here … sir, and how you got in?”

“Not at all, Captain. We suspected your electronic eye might be a bluff, so Lieutenant Harrington and I decided to call it.”

The captain exclaimed, “What! That’s impossible!”

“Don’t take my word for it, try it yourself.”

"I will."

Captain Barry personally crawled under the eye without setting off the alarm then he duck-stepped through, still no alarm. He walked through upright without as much as a peep, and as we left, he drove his vehicle back and forth across the *super protective* eye.

A couple of days later, Major Bensen asked me to participate in another scheme designed to test the security at the alert cells. This time, he took full credit for the idea and its success depended, not upon the faulty operation of some highly sophisticated system, but on human nature, an area in which the major had few peers.

He showed me his research: The base delivered a clean, and most importantly, empty, dipsy dumpster (a large, white garbage container) to the alert barn every Thursday morning at ten sharp. After dropping off the empty dumpster by hydraulic truck, the loaded one got taken to the base dump.

Half an hour before the scheduled arrival of the truck, we positioned ourselves in a wooded area on a bend in the dirt road leading to the barn. I helped the major pull a pile of brush and one big, dead, pine tree across the road.

As we waited, hidden in the bushes, he quipped, "This time try to be a little more careful."

Right on schedule the truck raced down the road, leaving a cloud of dust in its wake. I saw the bewildered look on the airman's face as he approached the pile of debris. He stopped short of the blockade and jumped out, lit a cigarette and slowly began removing the junk. At the precise moment, Major Bensen tugged on my flight suit and I followed him, quietly this time, to the rear of the truck and then into the empty dumpster.

The truck reached the guard shack and came to an abrupt stop. As Major Bensen anticipated, the AP guard opened the electrically controlled gate without bothering to inspect the dumpster. Once inside, the *white elephant* got gently placed at the side of the alert barn, right beside its bloated sister. We remained silent while the hydraulic truck lifted the other dumpster and then drove off. Then we waited for another half hour, carefully timing the routine of the AP on patrol. On one pass, he discarded an empty coke can which ricocheted around the hollow interior, knocking off the major's hat and evoking a muttered profanity.

At the calculated time, we climbed out and slid home free through a nearby door. Aircraft 400 sat in the cell. The major took a roll of masking tape from his knee pocket and put a small piece on the armament door, signing it with his initials. Then, one by one we visited the other birds standing alert, leaving our mark on each one, just in case Captain Barry had any doubts.

Afterward, Major Bensen asked around and then telephoned Captain Barry in the midst of a poker game. Only this time he refused to tell the good captain how we gained entry. Instead, he informed the APs on patrol and also the embarrassed, but very thankful guard at the gate.

Satisfied the air police guarding the alert barn had been made more aware of the devious and desperate techniques of sabotage, Major Bensen decided to direct some attention to the squadron area.

He remembered how the AP at the alert barn got rid of the coke when he saw Captain Barry coming and this gave him an idea. The major told me that each evening the base canteen van entered the squadron to dispense coffee and other goodies to the airmen working the night shift. He also knew that Captain Barry did not allow the APs to use the canteen van and therein saw an opportunity.

It took a little persuasion to convince the driver of the mobile canteen that the security of the entire United States depended upon his cooperation, but I never had doubt that the major would succeed.

So one evening, I found myself dressed in white coveralls and driving the van into the squadron. Major Bensen huddled in a corner near the rear door. I drove directly to the farthest bird on the line and stopped behind the tail.

The AP on patrol cautiously edged toward the van, and when he got within range, he asked, "See any officers around?"

I answered, "No, it's clear."

He came closer and asked, "Hey, you're new. Where's Fred?"

"Fred's sick tonight."

The AP said, "That goldbrick. Right now, he's probably swinging down at Falmouth."

"Probably … what'll it be?"

"Give me a hot dog and a coffee … black."

Clearing a path to the aircraft for Major Bensen, I said, "Sure, but go around to the other side. This side's busted."

While I served the AP, Major Bensen quietly opened the rear door and went to the aircraft and as I drove away I saw his dark form sitting motionless in the cockpit. I drove slowly around the apron watching as the AP resumed his patrol. As he passed near the cockpit, the major leaned over and said something quick, which looked like, "Boo." The frightened AP whirled around looking for the source of the voice. His rifle flew to the pavement and before he could retrieve his piece, the major stood up in the cockpit and identified himself. Then he spent the next half hour telling a group of APs about the potential wiles of the ORI team.

Labor Day weekend came and with it a definite nip in the air. Labor Day was nice and warm so Janice packed a lunch and we spent the entire day on a lonely stretch of beach north of Falmouth, reminiscing about the summer. It had been a hectic time for the squadron. Still Janice and I had managed to find time on weekends to be together. Best of all, I think we enjoyed driving along the curvy back roads and seeing the shingled cottages and interesting faces of the natives. The Cape seemed always so quaint and serene despite the hordes of tourists, and it seemed we always found some old museum or new candle shop, both of which fascinated Janice.

Geographically speaking, Cape Cod is one place, yet it is so majestically different. At the tip in Provincetown, the atmosphere is wild and artistic. The Hyannis area in the center of the Cape is basically conservative and sophisticated. Falmouth, closest to the base, had a young college flavor. Wherever we went, we always seemed to bump into someone or other from the squadron. In Hyannis, we usually ran into a married pilot or NCO and his family. The bachelor pilots and electronic types seemed to gravitate to Falmouth, while the crew chiefs invariably made the long journey up to Provincetown.

I have always been intrigued by the magic of the Kennedys, and Janice thought it amusing because I got such a thrill walking around the fenced-in Kennedy compound in Hyannis Port one day. Another time we visited the Oceanographic Institute at Woods Hole and even got permission to enter the deep diving bell. We had luck because the watchman happened to be a retired Air Force sergeant. That same afternoon, we took the ferry from Woods Hole to Martha's Vineyard and visited some places off the Cape too.

We spent a day in Boston, walking the narrow streets in the old section. On the way back to the Cape, we stopped at Plymouth, the landing spot of the Pilgrims, and promised each other that we would return during the Thanksgiving season. Once we visited the rough little fishing town of New Bedford and while there it seemed easy to imagine how it must have been in the old whaling days.

Our trips took us past many a seafood stand and I developed a liking for soft-shelled clams and stuffed quahogs, not to mention a pretty, blue-eyed blonde who sparkled in the fresh Cape Cod air.

In the middle of the next week, Janice and I had an experience with the air police we won't forget, and it turned out to be a memorable occasion for us in more ways than one. It had rained off and on that day, and I returned to the squadron in the evening to be with the night shift awhile. Janice went home after work and had supper, but remembered the colonel wanted the August flying report ready to go out first thing in the morning, so she decided to return to the squadron to pick up the material and type it at home.

While I watched several airmen replacing a strut on an aircraft, an airman rushed up to me and exclaimed, "Lieutenant, you better get over to Ops quick! An AP guard has Janice on the deck!"

I rushed through the hangar, into the pouring rain to Operations. I saw Janice, soaking wet and spread-eagled on the pavement with the AP guard in black raingear, pointing his rifle at her.

As I approached them, I heard her plead, "I'm Colonel Wyler's secretary. I'm here to pick up some typing."

The AP guard asked, "Once again, lady, do you have a clearance to be here?"

I went to Janice, knelt by her side and started to help her up as I looked at the AP, saying, "This is the colonel's secretary."

Pointing his rifle at us, the AP warned, "Hold it! She has to stay on the ground."

"I told you … she's the CO's secretary. Now let her go!"

"I can't. She doesn't have a badge. If I let her go, Captain Barry will have my ass. Okay, lady, get back down on the pavement!"

Janice screamed, "What! You're crazy!"

At that moment, an AP sergeant arrived on the scene, the light atop his station wagon flashing red.

Janice began sobbing. Her blonde hair, shining in the flashes of red light, appeared plastered to her face. A flower print, jersey dress seemed to be soaked through and glued to her curvaceous body.

Thankfully, the AP sergeant immediately recognized Janice and advised the guard to let her go then said, "The guard did his job, Lieutenant. Without her badge, she's an intruder."

I replied, "You better pray she doesn't catch pneumonia."

Janice explained to the AP sergeant how it happened. When she reached the squadron she found the front door locked. She said she pounded on the door to get the attention of the airman on duty in Operations, but apparently because of the hard rain he didn't hear her. She said at this point she made the bad decision to try to cross through a short span of the restricted zone to reach the rear door of Operations where she knew the airman worked. But as she rounded the corner, she heard the order to 'halt or be shot'.

With my arm around her, we entered the building and went straight to the colonel's office. I wanted to close the blinds on the big picture window, but on the way, I hit my shin on a low corner of a sleeping cot. Janice told me that Talifano delivered the cots during the week and the colonel opened his to get it ready for the ORI. My leg really hurt, so I sat on the cot.

Janice forgot about her own troubles and tried to console me. "Are you all right, Joe?"

"Yeah, but it smarts like hell."

I looked at her. An area light on the apron was our moon flowing through the big window. Streaks of radiance bounced off her wet hair and beautifully tanned face.

She looked like a goddess, and I said, "I love you, Janice."

"I love you too, Joe."

That's the first time we said that to each other and our lips met.

Afterward, we found a towel in a bag the colonel always kept ready. In the closet, we found a neatly pressed flight suit which fit Janice pretty well. I followed her home and had to laugh when the stunned AP at the main gate did a double take, seeing a pretty blonde in an orange flight suit with an eagle on the breast.

The flying report … we forgot about that.

Chapter 13
Gangbusters

On the evening of September 15, I received a strange phone call at the BOQ from Tech Sergeant Cummings at his bait shop. "I think something's up, Lieutenant."

"Oh? What's that, Sarge?"

"I talked to a couple of fishermen that just came in, and they said that two more Russian trawlers are moving into position."

"What do you suppose that means?"

"Could be the Russians know something, sir … like an ORI."

I immediately called Major Bensen at home.

"No doubt about it," he said. "They wouldn't miss this show for the world. You get in touch with Townley. I'll alert maintenance control and then see if I can convince Captain Barry to put some extra APs on duty after midnight. They'll probably hit us right before dawn."

ORI did start and began in the dark at the alert barn during the quiet hours before dawn. One member of the ORI team approached the AP at the gate and pretended to be one of the squadron pilots returning from an unauthorized night on the town. He pleaded with the AP airman to let him in before someone reported his absence.

The guard clamped on a pair of handcuffs.

Meanwhile, three ORI saboteurs attempted to sneak into the barn from the rear. One became hung up on the barbed wire fence and the other two got caught crawling on all fours toward the cells.

Later, an airman on duty in Operations told me what happened at the squadron. The ORI inspectors created a little diversion by having an apparent drunk drive his car onto the apron. Then, he acted loud and obnoxious and refused to spread-eagle. After Major Bensen's episodes, the APs weren't fooled and afterward captured four ORI members coming from the opposite direction, trying to get close enough to the birds to declare a successful sabotage.

The airman said, "Because the sabotage was unsuccessful, the ORI leader, a bald, beady-eyed colonel named Spencer, entered the squadron and produced the necessary clearances to free his men."

He said then Colonel Spence read from instructions ordering him to initiate the squadron recall plan to load all operationally ready aircraft with nuclear weapons. He also said Colonel Spencer asked him if he understood, and once he acknowledged that he did, the colonel started a stopwatch, marked the time on the document and had him sign his name, rank and serial number. Then he said the colonel just observed as he started down his checklist, first calling maintenance control. When the airman in maintenance control replied that he already knew about the ORI, and that all the birds sat on the line ready to be loaded, the colonel cursed and pounded a fist on the desk.

The airman then notified Colonel Wyler at home.

When the alarm sounded in the BOQ, I bolted out of bed, splashed water on my face, and crawled into my flight suit and boots. Within minutes, I joined the procession of cars heading for the squadron. Townley beat me in and I saw him making some last minute aircraft assignments. Without stopping, I signaled my presence and proceeded through the empty hangar and out to the apron. The line buzzed with air police vehicles moving back and forth, preparing to secure the load area as soon as everybody got in place. Crew chiefs and armament loading teams hurried to their assigned birds. For identification purposes the inspectors wore black arm bands and carried clipboards, and like flies they seemed to be everywhere.

I took my familiar position in front of the middle group of birds. A few minutes later Warrant Officer Shock arrived and waved a sleepy good morning. I noticed Major Bensen and Townley watching from the front of Hangar One, and when the nuclear convoy finally emerged on the far side of the apron, Townley jumped back into the pickup and the major headed for operations.

My birds loaded without incident and when Captain Roberts scurried by with a smile on his face, I knew the load had succeeded.

The word came to unload the Nukes and install the dummies in preparation for the first launch. While unloading a crack of thunder came from the other side of the base—the first alert bird scrambled.

Seconds later, four other alert birds blasted off in succession to meet the first wave of *enemy bombers*, probably an assortment of T-33s, F-4s, and other aircraft secretly prearranged and scheduled as targets for the ORI.

With my last bird safely unloaded, I joined Sergeant Townley in the pickup. The stark look on his rugged face gave an indication of the *battle* to come, surely some well conceived plan to test the capabilities of the airmen and durability of the aircraft. The sergeant moved down the line as the crew chiefs made their last minute flight checks. The pilots, already strapped in, awaited the *go* from Ops.

I asked, "What does the crew chief situation look like?"

"Good," Townley said. "We have five standing by to handle the alert birds when they return."

"I didn't even think of that. I guess we'll have all eighteen of our interceptors over here at the same time."

Townley said, "Yeah, could get hairy."

"How long do you think it'll last?"

"You never know … a day, several days … maybe a week."

"When I get a chance, I'll see if Major Bensen knows anything."

"Right. Oh, Lieutenant, I almost forgot. Control called during the load to tell everyone that we have to be careful with radio communications. The Russians are listening."

He no sooner got the words out when a call came over the radio: "Flight line one, this is Control."

The voice sounded like Sergeant Conn, but it had a different accent. It sounded a little suspicious, and strangely familiar.

Hesitating at first, Townley finally picked up the mike and said, "Go ahead, Control."

"Ops wants napalm loaded on the first three birds, flight line. The Russian trawlers are within our territorial limits."

Then it struck both of us at the same time … Airman Fritz … up to his old tricks. Townley jumped out of the truck and I called Control to reassure the real Sergeant Conn.

While Townley searched for Fritz, the first aircraft, 272, got the call to go. The pilot started the engine and the instant the crew chief pulled the chocks, it jumped out and headed for the runway. Next came 260, our *Hangar Queen*, and I thought back to Sergeant Taft's prediction: *She'll never fly again, Lieutenant.* Then 255, our *Black Sheep* from Sawyer, started up. Airman Bean yanked the chocks and ran to the front, signaling Lieutenant Commander Thompson to move out.

Returning to the truck, Townley gave a look which assured me we would hear no more of Airman Fritz. We watched as 272 and 260 began their rolls together.

Then Major Harmon started 400 and Townley said, "So far it looks pretty good."

When Captain Lickle started 280 next, the sergeant crossed his fingers for luck. As Major Harmon and Captain Lickle proceeded to the runway, Lieutenant Parks started 300. Then Colonel Wyler wound up *old 381*, but a moment later he signaled Airman Panza to come up to the cockpit.

Townley groaned, "Christ! He wouldn't be concerned about the windshield at a time like this, would he?"

I shrugged and the sergeant jumped out and climbed the ladder right behind Panza. The colonel pointed to the instrument panel with concern. I watched as Townley studied the panel. Then, shaking his head he gave the colonel a thumb down signal for an abort. Visibly upset, the colonel cut the power and yanked off his chin strap.

Hopping back in the truck, Townley said, "Oil pressure's way out and fluctuating. I'll have Panza tow the bird to hangar three and get Sergeant Singly on it right away."

Aircraft 300 lifted off and in the next ten minutes we watched 259, 415, 375, 385, and finally 378 with Lieutenant Holt, all get up. The launch had been good, certainly enough birds to meet whatever threat might be on the way in, providing, of course, the pilots made their intercepts and the birds held up in flight.

We didn't get much time to relax because as soon as 378 flew out of sight, Control called.

Grabbing the mike, Townley answered, "Go ahead, Control."

"The alert birds are on their way in, Sarge," Conn advised. "Ops would like them turned around and back up as soon as armament can unload the Nukes and get dummies on. Can you handle it?"

To make sure there would be no doubt in Conn's mind, and at the same time confuse the Russians, Townley answered, "Does a Russian bear shit in the woods?"

The first alert bird landed and the pilot told us that the Russian trawlers had lifted anchors and moved back. Apparently they had believed Fritz or didn't want to take any chances.

While Townley met the other incoming birds, Major Bensen came to the truck. "This exercise is a lot bigger than anybody anticipated. It's some kind of limited nuclear war thing and every squadron in ADC is involved. They're going to throw everything they can at us."

Thoroughly confused, I asked, "Limited nuclear war?"

Eyebrows raised, he said, "Yeah, don't ask me to explain what that means. It's some kind of new war philosophy going around these days. It's based on the idea that if both sides went after each other with missiles, there'd be total destruction with everybody wiped out immediately. So instead, a limited nuclear war makes a contest out of it; still a nuclear war, but with both sides using bombers and interceptors until somebody gains an advantage."

"I see."

"Good, because I'm not sure I do. But anyway, it means this could last a long time so get ready. That scramble of the alert birds was to intercept the first wave of *Russian bombers*. They'll be coming at us for quite some time, probably right through the night. I wonder how they arranged for all the targets without us finding out about 'em?"

"During the load, four ORI pilots took off in our T-Birds."

"Yeah, I know. That's standard. Well, I have to brief Will Shock and maintenance control yet. Once you get these birds back up, you and Townley should have a few minutes to plan your shifts."

"Okay."

The major started to walk away then stopped and said, "You know, I think we'll have enough problems without asking the men to fight a limited war."

"I got you," I said and he hurried toward Hangar Two.

Somehow Rosy got wind of the limited nuclear war business and bugged Sergeant Taft so much that the sergeant made an unprecedented visit to the line to talk to me.

I asked, "What's bothering him?"

"He says that radioactive fallout will kill everybody anyway, limited or not."

"To tell you the truth, Sarge, I'm not sure how all that works."

Sergeant Taft shrugged and headed back to face Rosy. I thought, at least it was a break for Sergeant Taft.

If war is hell, I'm not sure how to describe a limited war. But without letup, the birds flew through that first day and right through the night. The weather seemed to be in our favor and one crew chief made the obvious, but until then, unthought-of suggestion, that all maintenance be performed right on the line instead of towing the birds into the hangars. So, at night we set up mobile floodlights on the line.

We split our people into two twelve hour shifts and isolated one section of the flight line lounge by hanging parachutes across the room, hoping this would make it possible for the off shift to get some sleep, but it didn't work out that way. Shortly after dark, transient aircraft began coming in and we had to get every available man out to the line. The number of aircraft needing service outnumbered the men and some crew chiefs had to take care of two and three birds at a time. Airman Buckley remained too valuable to put on a bird and during the hectic period, he saved us more than once by providing parts, supposedly unavailable at base supply. I figured Buckley must have had a warehouse somewhere, but at any rate, Sergeant Townley really learned to appreciate the fruits of *self-actualization.* In all the confusion, the flight chiefs performed the functions of crew chiefs, and I even managed to refuel several birds.

Sergeant Townley's effort seemed unequaled. The sergeant somehow managed to meet each aircraft as it landed. Quickly but surely he debriefed each pilot then called maintenance control and outlined the work to be accomplished, telling Control what shop to send out and when they should report. Sergeant Townley said the crew chiefs got a taste of the *old days* because they had firm control of the work taking place on their birds and made a lot of important decisions.

The maintenance airmen even appreciated Sergeant Talifano because the first sergeant kept the box lunches coming and the coffee hot. I saw Major Bensen on line doing his thing, providing inspiration and making sure each airman knew what his contribution meant to our success. The major's presence paid off directly in one respect. During the busy night-time period, several transient pilots became upset because they had to wait longer than normal to get their birds serviced. They started giving the struggling crew chiefs a bad time.

Major Bensen stepped in and informed the visitors. "In the 50th, crew chiefs are treated with the utmost respect."

Our own pilots knew better than to hassle the crew chiefs. Even Colonel Wyler, who suffered through four consecutive aborts with 381, knew better than to vent his frustration on Airman Panza.

The transients left us before dawn, and as the sun rose on the second day, I saw the tired, but still determined faces of the airmen. A respite didn't take place and the flying continued on through the morning hours. By noon, Sergeant Townley looked ragged (not to mention how I felt) and the expression on his face seemed grim as he showed me the status of the birds—only eight in commission. Of those out of commission, three had serious radar problems and Will Shock estimated four hours at the earliest. Three more needed extensive engine work and Sergeant Singly estimated four hours to get those back in commission. Of the remaining four birds only one, with a cylinder leak, seemed a possible within the next three hours.

The situation looked really bleak when Control called.

Townley answered, "Go ahead, Control."

"Eight birds at 12:30 flight line."

We could provide eight, but no more.

Drawing a breath, Townley said, "Roger, Control, we got them."

Sergeant Conn answered, "Good."

Major Bensen came out to watch the eight birds get off and afterward, I followed him back to the pilots' mess.

We found Colonel Wyler pleading with the ORI chief. "It's not fair. You're just trying to fly us into the ground."

Colonel Spencer snapped, "Everything's fair in war."

Major Bensen didn't restrain himself and said, "Since when is it the custom to keep flying without giving maintenance time to fix the aircraft?"

With a snicker, Colonel Spencer said, "You'll get your chance … if you make it through the next launch."

His words sounded like an omen and I had the feeling he knew about our predicament: We only had the eight birds flying which would be available for the next launch if they all got down okay, but like the morning flights, we expected at least four to return out of commission. The cocky look in Spencer's eyes also assured us that at least eight *enemy* targets had already been scheduled for the final launch of the day.

Sergeant Townley would have called it a miracle if all eight birds came back in commission. One by one, we met the eight birds as they returned. Confirming our fears, after we assessed them, we only had four available for the last launch.

Ten minutes later, Sergeant Conn called and told us Operations called for eight birds in twenty minutes.

Townley replied, "We'll give you four."

"Huh? Okay, we'll take four … out."

Fully anticipating the end of ORI for the 50th, I said, "I guess that's it, Sarge."

"Don't feel too bad about it, Lieutenant. Everybody did their best. We almost made it. What the hell does the Air Force expect from an old, tired bird anyway?"

Just then four ORI pilots came out of operations and began walking toward our T-Birds to be used as target aircraft.

"Look at that," Townley said. "They sure know how to rub it in, using our own birds for the kill. Oh hell, I guess it won't hurt to give them a lift."

After Townley pulled the pickup over, the pilots hopped on the back with their gear. Tech Sergeant Cummings and Airman Swartz waited at the T-Birds and greeted the *enemy* pilots with smiles. Like good bellhops, they helped the pilots carry their gear to the respective T-Birds.

Townley drove off and dropped me off at operations.

In the mess, Colonel Wyler, Major Harmon, and Major Bensen sat together, looking depressed and drinking coffee in silence. At the next table, several lively ORI inspectors talked with a happy looking Colonel Spencer. I filled my cup and sat in an empty chair between Major Bensen and the colonel. Fifteen minutes passed with hardly a word spoken.

Then Sergeant Townley appeared, waving in the doorway. At this stage, it almost seemed like an apparition. I walked over to him.

"What's up, Sarge?"

Smiling, Townley whispered, "Our four T-Birds just aborted, Lieutenant."

"What! All four? How did that happen?"

Townley shuffled his feet. "They all had engine overheat lights come on before they even got off the apron," he explained, the only time I ever saw him happy about an abort.

I tried hard to subdue my own pleasure and asked again, "All four? How did that happen?"

"Coincidence, I guess, sir. Well, I have to get back to the line. You better ask Cummings, Lieutenant."

Returning to the table, I whispered the new development to Major Bensen. I thought his eyes were going to pop out.

A moment later, one of the ORI pilots rushed into the mess and quickly briefed Colonel Spencer.

The ORI chief immediately turned pale then pointing a finger at Colonel Wyler, he yelled, "Of all the low-down, dirty tricks! You put those T-Birds out of commission on purpose!"

Colonel Wyler, still unaware of the reason for Spencer's rage, looked toward Major Bensen.

The major first shrugged his shoulders then looking directly at Colonel Spencer said, "All's fair in war … remember, Colonel?"

Hurrying from the mess, followed by the other ORI members, the ORI chief proclaimed, "Well tomorrow's another day."

Tech Sergeant Cummings never volunteered any explanation for the mysterious overheat condition which conveniently grounded the four *enemy bombers* just when all seemed hopelessly lost. And as far as I know, Townley never asked him either. The problem couldn't have been too serious though, because within two hours the status board in the flight line lounge showed all four T-Birds back in commission.

That gave us until dawn to fix the birds and get ready for the next phase of the ORI. The pilots and ORI inspectors left for a good night's sleep and a light rain began to fall. The NCOs met in the little narrow conference room in Hangar Two and planned all the work that needed to be accomplished. We had an unusual rash of engine problems during the last twelve hours and Sergeant Singly had a lot to accomplish during the night. Five birds were scheduled for trim pad runs then they would be given to radar. During the day, several crew chiefs nursed hydraulic leaks and the cylinders needed to be repacked or changed. Every bird exceeded the number of landings allowed per tire and every tire had to be changed. Captain Lickle's hard landing ripped the skin of 378, so Sergeant Jones would do his thing on that bird, and if it had been any other pilot but Captain Lickle, Jones would have graciously accepted the challenge.

About midnight, we received our first battle report, coming in by Sergeant Talifano. Sergeant Townley and I sat in my office going over the status of each aircraft when Talifano entered from the hangar, looking fresh as a daisy in his immaculate dress blues. Tired and struggling to keep awake, Sergeant Townley gave a low growl as the first sergeant proceeded to the bulletin board. In the lounge, most of the crew chiefs rested or slept on cots, trying desperately to catch a few winks. Talifano tacked up a sheet of paper and hurried out the door.

I saw from my office, that of all the crew chiefs, only Airman Bean mustered the energy to get up and walk to the board.

Half asleep, I heard him call out, "Get a load of this."

One of the other airmen asked from his cot, "What's up, Bean?"

Another demanded, "Yeah, read us the news."

Bean read the Bulletin, "Northern sector sustains heavy losses. Chicago, Detroit, Saint Paul-Minneapolis, all destroyed. Eighty-ninth Fighter Interceptor Squadron incapacitated."

Someone asked, "Inca … what?"

Bean added, "Incapacitated, dummy … knocked out … finished … done."

"Hoo-ray," a crew chief yelled, followed by a resounding cheer from the others.

"Oh, yeah, listen to this," Bean read: "Remaining Sixty-Ninth aircraft to be diverted to Fiftieth at Olefield."

A series of boos erupted and Sergeant Townley rushed to the board to make sure Bean read it right.

Someone asked, "What about us, Bean? Are we still alive?"

"Yeah, here it is," Bean said. "Northeast sector sustains only minor damage thus far. Boston destroyed."

A crew chief inquired, "Who the hell missed their intercept?"

Townley took a guess. "Probably Captain Lickle."

Bean added, "Here's the rest. Other metropolitan areas in the northeast survive, but a major assault can be expected in the morning."

Major Bensen called from Operations close to three in the morning. "Joe, I'm with the colonel. What's the latest on 381?"

"I think it's out on the engine trim pad right now. I'm about to go out to the line. I'll check and get right back to you."

"Okay."

I walked through the busy hangar and stopped at the entrance, the rain coming down hard. Within minutes, Sergeant Townley pulled over and I jumped in.

"It looks pretty good, Lieutenant. So far we've got twelve ready. By dawn I think we might have about fifteen."

"Good. What about Three-eighty-one (381)?"

"Depolo's on the trim pad right now. If the engine checks out, we'll be in great shape."

"I hope it does because he's climbing the walls since he's not flying like he hoped to."

"Yeah, well, Depolo should be starting her up any second now."

The truck radio gave a few squeaks. "Control, this is the pad."

"Go ahead, pad," Control responded.

From his vehicle far out at the trim pad, Depolo said, "Request permission to start and run Three-eighty-one (381)."

"Roger … permission granted pad."

Chapter 14

Final Approach

We heard the loud roar of the engine out on the trim pad.

Listening as Depolo ran the engine at low speed, Townley said, "Sounds pretty good."

Depolo took it up to full power then brought it back to idle.

Sergeant Townley looked satisfied with the way the engine sounded so I said, "I think the colonel's getting his bird after all."

"Yeah, sounds that way," Townley said.

Once again Depolo applied power and came back to idle, only this time the engine shut down.

Townley exclaimed, "What the hell! I better call and tell him to give that bird a better run than that."

We waited, giving Depolo time to get out of 381 and back into his vehicle. But to our surprise the engine started again.

Sergeant Townley said, "I wonder what's going on out there?"

"I don't know … strange."

As Depolo took 381 through the power ranges, Townley said, "I better find out what's going on. Control, this is Flight line one."

"You're on, Flight line."

"I need to talk to Depolo. Have Ops get in touch with him in the cockpit and tell him to shut that bird down and call me."

"Roger, Flight line … will do."

A minute later the engine stopped and Sergeant Depolo called, "Flight line one, this is the pad. Come in."

Townley asked, "Why did you shut that engine down the first time?"

Depolo said, "That's a mistake Sarge. Everything's fine now."

"What kind of mistake?"

"It's not that important, Sarge. I guess I brought the throttle back too hard and forced it past the detent."

"Wait there," Townley ordered. "I'm on my way out."

"Roger, Sarge … out."

Townley and I drove out to the pad where Depolo waited in the truck. Without stopping to discuss the problem, Townley climbed the ladder and hopped into the cockpit. I followed and peered in the cockpit from the ladder as he jockeyed the throttle back and forth, moving it outboard, then back in, between idle and full power. Then, the throttle slipped past the detent and into the stop position.

Townley exclaimed, "See that!"

"Yeah, what happened?"

"I don't know. Let's see if I can do it again."

Again he moved the throttle through its full range. And each time he brought the throttle back, the detent stopped the throttle just as it's supposed to. Once again, as Townley brought the throttle back with what looked like very little pressure, it slipped through the detent and into the stop position. When it happened, it shocked both of us and we just looked at each other.

I saw the puzzled expression on the sergeant's face and asked, "What could be the problem?"

"We won't know until we take the throttle assembly apart, but first let's try it with the engine running."

Sergeant Townley started the engine and worked the throttle for several minutes, the same as a pilot would do on final approach, with steady but easy pressure, and each time the detent did its job, preventing the throttle from moving into the stop engine position. He tried again and again, looking through the windshield to simulate actual flight. Everything worked fine with the engine running. Townley persisted in working the throttle.

I didn't expect anything, but then it happened again. The throttle slipped through the detent and the engine shut down with a whine.

Townley screamed, "That's it! That's what happened to Captain Seimons and those other birds!"

Also excited, I said, "They didn't have a chance. No time for an air start if that happens on final."

"That's for sure. Now we have to find out why."

In less than half an hour, Sergeant Depolo had the throttle assembly out of 381 and resting on a table in the flight line lounge. Word spread quickly and it looked like half of maintenance gathered around as Townley, with the skill of a surgeon, proceeded to open the assembly. With the cover plates removed, he slowly moved the throttle while at the same time observing the detent assembly, a mechanism with a spring-held steel ball. The ball, about the size of a marble, sat firmly in the spring. When the throttle arm made contact with the ball it fulfilled its purpose, stopping any further backward movement of the throttle, unless sufficient and conscious pressure got applied to depress the spring, thereby allowing the throttle to pass through into the Stop Engine position.

Like everybody else in front, I watched each time Townley moved the throttle back, making contact with the steel ball, and each time the throttle arm stopped, but with each contact the ball seemed to move ever so slightly on its seat. After one bump the ball moved a little more and centered itself such that a badly worn and corroded section of its surface became exposed.

I could see the corrosion clearly and Sergeant Townley saw it too. He moved the throttle back with gentle pressure and with only a slight, scraping resistance the arm slid through and into the Stop Engine position.

A pained expression came to Sergeant Townley's face and he muttered, "Why didn't I think of that sooner?"

Shaking my head I said, "It's not covered in any of the maintenance manuals."

"I know," Townley said, "but it will be from now on."

The sergeant took a screwdriver and pried the ball and spring loose then holding the ball between two fingers, he said, "Just look at that corrosion."

I saw one side looked discolored and somewhat worn.

Sounding disgusted, Townley said, "Look at that … special steel, guaranteed not to pit, wear, or corrode."

The other onlookers started buzzing about the discovery.

One of the airmen spoke up, "That's why they send old birds to the deserts of Arizona, Sarge."

Townley sighed, "I guess." Then he checked his watch. "We only got an hour before dawn. You better get this over to Major Bensen, Lieutenant. I'll get the flight chiefs started checking on the other birds."

"Okay. Cripes, I forgot about the major. He's probably still with the colonel waiting for the status report on Three-eighty-one (381)."

I carried the throttle assembly to the pilots' mess. Major Bensen and Major Harmon sat at a corner table drinking coffee as Colonel Wyler paced back and forth in stocking feet. The cooks started to make preparations for breakfast.

The throttle revelation caused quite a stir and Major Harmon went upstairs to wake Captain Lickle, sleeping on a cot in the hallway. The captain got up and immediately went into Operations to send emergency reports to all other squadrons, ADC headquarters, and Air Force headquarters.

Colonel Spencer arrived in the crowded mess and in light of the new discovery, everyone speculated about the ORI continuing. Colonel Wyler, Major Harmon, Captain Lickle, Major Bensen, and Spencer went back and forth between the mess and Operations, apparently discussing the matter with higher headquarters. The decision finally came that the ORI would continue as soon as all squadrons received the information. The pilots would be briefed on the danger and once aware, they could guard against inadvertently moving the throttle into the Stop Engine position.

Calling for everyone's attention, Colonel Wyler asked the pilots to gather in the conference room. Then Sergeant Townley walked into the mess with another throttle assembly in hand. Without saying a word, he handed the assembly to Major Bensen.

Colonel Wyler asked, "What bird is that out of?"

The major replied, "Old Two-fifty-one (251)."

"What! That bird crashed! How come it's still around?"

As the pilots looked on, Major Bensen inspected the exposed throttle and said, "We weren't able to arrange for a flatbed yet. And it looks like this throttle also has a corroded ball." Rising from his chair, the major announced, "Well, I have to make a trip."

The CO asked, "A trip? Where?"

"To Boston, to see Airman Tiddyings."

"What! Who?"

Major Harmon said, "That's the airman in the hospital sir … the boy who had the problem after the investigation."

Remembering, the colonel replied, "Oh, yes … Tiddyings. Well, I think Sergeant Talifano can handle that. I'll send him."

Major Bensen picked up the throttle assembly and firmly stated, “No, I’m going.”

“Now, wait a minute, Major. You can’t leave. You’re chief of maintenance.”

Major Bensen started for the door and said, “I’ll be back as soon as possible.”

The colonel yelled, “Harry, wait! I said no, and that’s an order!”

But the major kept walking and the colonel pursued him into the hallway. “Harry! Stop! I’ll have you court-martialed! We’re in the middle of a war.”

I guess nothing would have stopped Major Bensen, and we heard the colonel scream from the doorway, “It’s desertion, Harry!”

There was a long moment of dead silence in the mess then a deafening cheer arose, celebrating Major Bensen’s determination.

With Major Bensen on his way to Boston, the ORI once again began in earnest. Someone said Colonel Spencer had been up all night arranging with ADC Headquarters to hit us with everything he could get. On the first launch, we got fourteen aircraft off without a single abort and Sergeant Townley considered the feat a record. Even Colonel Wyler flew for the first time in 381.

The first bird returned an hour later, and Lieutenant Harris explained the problem even before he got out of the cockpit. “The ground-based radars are all knocked out.” Then pointing at the onboard radar he yelled, “Luckily, I found the target with this.”

The extent of the crisis became apparent once the other birds came down. Several pilots, unable to locate targets without ground radar, completely missed their intercepts and nine of the aircraft sat out of commission with radars out.

Warrant Officer Shock couldn’t believe it had happened and when Operations called for twelve aircraft *in one hour*. Will exclaimed, “That’s impossible … the most I can have ready is four!”

Sergeant Townley and I felt helpless when Sergeant Grobly, the A-Flight chief, came running over to the pickup.

Speaking to Townley, he said, “Give me a whack at them birds.”

Looking at Grobly like something might be wrong with him, Townley asked, “What birds?”

Breathing hard, Grobly said, “The ones out for radar.”

Townley shot back, “What the hell do you know about radars?”

"My boys have been living with them eggheads for eight months now. Fixing radars isn't really that complicated, once you find the right black box."

Sergeant Townley didn't answer.

Grobly persisted. "Bean's familiar with all radar test equipment. We could have those boxes out of the birds and tested in no time. Radar doesn't have enough people."

Still no answer from Townley, but I could see him giving the idea serious consideration.

I asked, "What do we have to lose? There's no going on without those birds for the next launch."

Townley grumbled, "Okay, what the hell … go ahead."

Grobly hurried off to round up his crew chiefs.

A-Flight had the boxes out and tested before Will Shock even knew it happened, and when Grobly reported five radars fixed before the radar technicians had their four ready, Will looked absolutely flabbergasted and said to Townley, "You guys fixed the five easy ones."

"Oh yeah," Townley shot back. "Why didn't you fix them first, then? You knew we needed the birds."

Will stammered, "Well, yeah," then hurried back to his hangar.

We made the launch and for the balance of the morning everything went fine, almost too fine. Then early in the afternoon the birds returned from one flight with a rash of malfunctions. Only this time it wasn't anything specific like radar, but a lot of different discrepancies like cylinder leaks, nose wheel shimmies, fuel transfer problems, and other symptoms of old age. And to compound the problem, many of the aircraft needed parts no longer available.

Townley and I rushed around the line, going from aircraft to aircraft, trying to help the crew chiefs make impossible repairs.

Still seven birds shy, Airman Panza reported his aircraft, old 381, back in commission.

Townley exclaimed, "That's impossible! How did you fix a fuel control?"

Panza replied, "I didn't. Buckley gave me one."

"What?"

"Yeah, Sarge. Buckley has all the parts we need in the lounge."

Townley and I rushed to the lounge. Sure enough, Buckley had a large assortment of parts, all spread out on the floor in one corner.

Recognizing his own handwriting on the green tags, Townley declared, “These parts are all from Two-fifty-one (251)!”

Airman Buckley said, “You checked them all out yourself, Sarge. They’re all good.”

“I know, but … but we can’t use parts from a crashed bird.”

Buckley argued, “We found the problem with Two-fifty-one (251), Sarge.”

Townley just looked at the parts, so nice and neat—cylinders, seals, generators, panels, all kinds of little motors and actuators, two new tires, valves and fittings, various instruments, and all certified operable and properly tagged by himself.

He drew a deep breath and decided. “Use them!”

The crew chiefs made a mad shuffle for the remaining parts.

As the afternoon wore on, Major Bensen had still not returned from Boston. Sergeant Townley and I wondered what the next crisis would be. One thing seemed certain, Colonel Spencer had more surprises to come.

Before the birds started coming back from a launch, Sergeant Conn called, “Ops wants quick turnarounds on all aircraft.”

Townley answered, “Roger, Control,” then pulled out to tell the flight chiefs.

One by one the aircraft came in and the crew chiefs turned them around. But an hour later, our birds came back again, only this time interspersed with other aircraft—ten Darts from Sawyer, some National Guard F-100s, and what looked like a whole squadron of F-101s. We put every available man on the line, but we needed more crew chiefs than we had. Right then, five radar flight technicians working out of the flight line hangar, came to the truck and volunteered to try to turn around aircraft.

Sergeant Townley looked dumbfounded and reluctantly said, “Well, go ahead, but if you guys have any problems just yell.”

The help from radar made the difference and we managed to get all the aircraft turned around in time to meet the next wave of targets. But when the birds began returning, it became apparent that even more assistance would be needed for the next launch. Colonel Spencer had made *some arrangements*, and Sergeant Townley and I counted fifty interceptors on the ground with more coming in and all had to be quickly turned around. It looked like a lot of birds would have to wait, allowing *enemy* targets to get through.

Then, quite suddenly, Sergeant Townley declared, "Well, hell, if radar can turn around birds so can a lot of other people!"

Townley jumped from the pickup and headed for the hangars.

Minutes later, strange faces began to swarm out to the line, airmen, like Sergeant Taft and Airman Rosenberg from supply, Sergeant Jones from sheet metal, Sergeant Singly and his boys from the engine shop, and even more radar technicians. I thought I recognized one of the cooks from the pilots' mess dressed in green fatigues, so I quickly surveyed the line to make sure no civilians got into the act. Of all people, I spotted Sergeant Talifano, still in his dress blues, putting fuel into one of the transient F-100s. Later, I learned that Talifano didn't exactly volunteer … he ran into Townley in Hangar Two.

It was all over when Major Bensen returned from Boston with a smiling, happy Airman Tiddyings, carrying the throttle assembly in one hand. First, they walked through all the hangars and when Tiddyings headed back to the communications shop, I followed the major into the mess. Colonel Wyler looked ecstatic about successfully completing the ORI and he acted like the earlier encounter with the major never happened.

The colonel greeted Major Bensen with open arms, and exclaimed, "We did it, Harry! We won!"

Looking toward a dejected Colonel Spencer, sulking in the corner, Major Bensen replied, "Oh, I always knew we would, sir."

That evening Major Bensen, Sergeant Townley, and I sat in the flight line lounge drinking coffee, and the major said, "Well, that's my last ORI."

With a sigh of relief, Townley said, "Me too. They're all yours from now on, Lieutenant."

I replied, "That's what I'm afraid of."

The major took a long, final swallow and then, looking directly into my eyes, said, "Just remember, Joe, it's each man that makes the difference."

Epilogue

In December, after thirty years of service, Major Bensen retired from the United States Air Force. One month later to the day, Chief Master Sergeant Townley followed suit. I realize now, I had the pleasure of working with two very special individuals and true maintenance professionals.

The squadron buzzed about the likelihood of a truce in Vietnam and what it all meant. Secretary of State, Kissinger declared, 'Peace is at hand'. Rosy, our political science expert, told the airmen in supply to disregard the peace scenario. In late December, he gained in stature as the bombing of North Vietnam intensified with Operation Linebacker.

In January, I made first lieutenant, but the real excitement in the squadron came with a possible truce in Southeast Asia. With the war winding down, changes came quickly. In February, Colonel Wyler held another commander's briefing and made the astonishing announcement that the flying quota would be reduced to a mere token of what we had been flying. The colonel explained that our country had an energy crisis and needed to conserve scarce natural resources. Rosy didn't buy that one either, and said that with the action in Vietnam slowing and the presidential election past, ADC no longer needed to prove anything to dissenting politicians.

The real shocker came in July 1973. We learned that Aerospace Defense Command merged into Continental Air Defense Command and this meant that ADC no longer existed—in theory anyway.

Then the airmen and NCOs started returning from Vietnam and the squadron crawled with new people. On the flight line we provided each bird with two crew chiefs, a luxury Townley would have dearly loved to see. With the flying drastically reduced, our biggest problem became keeping people busy.

One returning veteran summed it up: "It's either hurry up or wait, Lieutenant."

Janice and I tied the knot in early 1974 and after a honeymoon in Bermuda, the Air Force announced severe cutbacks. My notification came within a month, but my discharge got delayed because the base supply officer at Olefield refused, at first, to take custody of a million dollar fire truck.

Rosy said anyone could read the 'writing on the wall' and it meant ballistic missiles and submarines for air defense.

Janice and I moved to Pennsylvania where I found a job as supervisor in a small toy manufacturing company. After my time in the squadron, the work didn't seem very interesting.

In less than a year, we became the proud parents of twin boys. A year later on one of our frequent trips to Cape Cod to visit her parents, I decided to visit the squadron. It surprised me to find Sergeant Talifano, the big first sergeant, still there and he graciously arranged my security clearance and agreed to serve as my escort.

The sergeant hadn't changed a bit and he told me that as a *short-timer*, he would be retiring in two months.

I asked about Colonel Wyler and he gave me a serious look and said, "You mean General Wyler, Lieutenant. He's in Colorado Springs running things now."

Talifano said Major Bensen still lived on the Cape and had a thriving real estate business, and that he stopped in occasionally, especially if he could help some young airman with housing.

We took a quick tour through the squadron. Some of the faces looked familiar, but most of the people I knew had left. Warrant Officer Shock retired and Captain Roberts had been transferred, but nobody could remember where. Lieutenant Commander Thompson made full commander and returned to the Navy.

I asked about Lieutenants Holt and Parks and Talifano assured me they remained confirmed bachelors. Major Harmon remained as the operations officer and I forgot to ask about Captain Lickle, the colonel's eager henchman. I caught a look at the new squadron commander. Talifano said he came from Tactical Air Command and flew F-105s in Vietnam. The picture window remained.

On the flight line, Master Sergeant Grobly ran things now and the flight line officer slot remained vacant since I left. No one heard from Sergeant Townley who retired to South Carolina. I said hello to Airman Panza and Sergeant Cummings and learned that Airman Buckley, our scrounger, and alias *Scarecrow One*, had signed up for another hitch and had been transferred to Hawaii. But it saddened me very much to hear that Airman Bean got killed the summer before in a tragic automobile accident on the Cape.

Hangar Two crawled with electronic technicians and Talifano explained that in the past two years the old *Six* had been modified three more times with extensive electronic system changes.

On the way back to operations, we briefly looked in Maintenance Control. The room looked much larger, expanded twice since I left. Sergeant Conn sat at a monitor in one corner and I spoke to him briefly. Control looked crowded now, and I saw two master sergeants and several ominous computers demanding their attention.

Throughout my visit, I kept hearing talk of the 50th becoming a National Guard squadron.

That's the last time I went back to Olefield, but I often think of the scarecrow season past and what I came to know of the vast potential and capabilities of ordinary people. Most importantly, I learned that average human beings, if given enough individual freedom, will not only accept responsibility but seek it. Airman Buckley is a dramatic case in point, but there were many others, less conspicuous, but no less important. I came to realize that the spirit of any organization rests upon maintaining the basic importance and dignity of each man.

But lurking in every organization are deadly enemies of the human spirit. Oppressive power must be subdued, and sophisticated systems and technology, if unchallenged, will tend to make important people seem pretty useless.

I learned an atmosphere must be maintained so men can have some say in the decisions which affect the outcome of their work. Acceptance of such an atmosphere takes real conviction, because one must be prepared to accept the inevitability of some human error, but only through mistakes and some trial and error will people learn to grow and do their thing. Therein lies the key to personal satisfaction and solid contributions for any organization.

Major Benson said, "Our country received the ideas, ingenuity, and creativity of its most valuable resource … ordinary people."

I guess if you get right down to it, that's really the only difference between us and the Russians.

About the Author

Jack Verneski

Jack grew up in Nanticoke, Pennsylvania and graduated from Nanticoke High School. He entered the Navy as a seaman and received a Secretary of the Navy appointment to the U.S. Naval Academy, Annapolis, Maryland, where he graduated in 1962.

He then served in the U.S. Air Force as a maintenance officer in a fighter interceptor squadron and as a member of an Air Force accident investigation team.

After serving four years, he worked in military avionic sales at Bendix Corporation for several years and in marketing management for Penna Power & Light Co., Allentown, Pennsylvania. While there he received his MBA degree with a major in Management Science from Wilkes College, Wilkes-Barre, Pennsylvania.

Jack and his wife Joyce of 49 years live in Estero, Florida and have one daughter, Apolla, born during the moon landing, and two grandchildren.

Jack Verneski

Made in the USA
Charleston, SC
10 December 2012